...ly what was making her so nervous.

Plus the fact that Michael Finn was a high-flyer and she had never connected with anyone from his level of society. She was definitely out of his league in any social sense, and more than likely he only wanted a sexual fling with her—which she might as well accept right now and not get herself in a twist about it.

Regardless of his intentions she wanted to be with him, wanted to experience him, so no way was she going to back off at this point. Besides, a Cinderella could win a prince. Miracles could happen. Failing that, if the worst came to the worst she could write off her time with him as a case of real lust being satisfied—because while she had certainly fancied other guys in the past it had not been like this, not nearly as strongly as this. Michael Finn had her in an absolute tizzy of lust.

THE LEGENDARY FINN BROTHERS

Australia's most eligible billionaires!

THE INCORRIGIBLE PLAYBOY

January 2013

Everyone has heard about **Harry Finn**'s reputation:
he's utterly ruthless in the pursuit of
beautiful women, and his devilishly charming smile
is virtually irresistible! What he wants, he gets—
and top of his list is secretary Elizabeth Flippence…

HIS MOST EXQUISITE CONQUEST

July 2013

Notorious for being merciless in the boardroom,
tycoon **Michael Finn** is all work and no play.
Distractions aren't on his agenda—
especially in the too-tempting shape of bubbly,
beautiful Lucy Flippence…

HIS MOST EXQUISITE CONQUEST

BY
EMMA DARCY

First published in Great Britain 2013
by Mills & Boon, an imprint of Harlequin (UK) Limited.
Harlequin (UK) Limited, Eton House, 18-24 Paradise Road,
Richmond, Surrey TW9 1SR

ISBN: 978 0 263 90021 7

Harlequin (UK) policy is to use papers that are natural, renewable and recyclable products and made from wood grown in sustainable forests. The logging and manufacturing process conform to the legal environmental regulations of the country of origin.

Printed and bound in Spain
by Blackprint CPI, Barcelona

Initially a French/English teacher, **Emma Darcy** changed careers to computer programming before the happy demands of marriage and motherhood. Very much a people person, and always interested in relationships, she finds the world of romance fiction a thrilling one, and the challenge of creating her own cast of characters very addictive.

Recent titles by the same author:

THE INCORRIGIBLE PLAYBOY
  (The Legendary Finn Brothers)
AN OFFER SHE CAN'T REFUSE
THE COSTARELLA CONTRACT
HIDDEN MISTRESS, PUBLIC WIFE

CHAPTER ONE

A DEARLY BELOVED daughter buried in the wrong plot.

A man digging up a grave.

A dog running amok in the memorial garden, knocking off angels' heads.

What a Monday morning, Lucy Flippence thought as she drove to Greenlands Cemetery, having been given the job of dealing with these situations. Just when some slack time would have been very handy, too, it being her sister's birthday. It would be really nice to take Ellie out to lunch, especially since Lucy was dying to see her in the wildly colourful new clothes with the new hairdo.

It would be like a complete makeover and highly due, given it was Ellie's thirtieth birthday. For the past two years her sister had been drowning in blacks and greys and taupes, and so caught up in being Michael Finn's personal assistant, she didn't have any other life—not one man sparking her interest.

Right now Lucy had quite a fresh understanding of this disinterest in men. The nasty incident in the Irish pub at Port Douglas had spoiled her weekend away with friends. The guy had started out a promising prince and turned into a horrid frog. It seemed to her they all did, sooner or later. At twenty-eight she had yet to meet one whose shining armour remained shiny, regardless of circumstances.

Even so, she wasn't about to give up on men. She enjoyed the exciting high of a new attraction, loved the sense of being loved, if only for a little while. It was worth the hurt of being disillusioned. As long as she lived, she was going to be out there, experiencing everything that looked and felt good. It was what her mother had told her to do—her mother who'd married her horrible frog father because she was pregnant with Ellie.

'Don't ever make that mistake, Lucy. Be careful.'

She was.

Always careful.

Especially since she didn't want to have children, didn't want to pass on her dyslexia, blighting another life with it. Putting a child through what she'd been through at school was not an act of love, and the problems didn't stop there, either. The incurable disability blocked a heap of avenues that normal people simply took in their stride.

The thought of an innocent baby being born with a wrongly wired brain like hers triggered a strongly negative recoil inside Lucy. She would not risk that happening. Which meant, of course, she would probably never marry—no real point to it if having a family was out of the question.

There was, however, always the hope of meeting a prince who didn't care about having children, or perhaps one who had a genetic fault of his own and would be happy to simply settle with having each other to love. She hadn't ruled out these possibilities. They bolstered her resolve to keep moving on, making the most of her journey through life.

The cemetery on the outskirts of Cairns came into view. It was aptly named Greenlands—everything being so very green as it usually was up here in far north tropical Queensland, especially after the big wet and before the oppressive heat of summer. August was always a pleasant month and Lucy was glad she wasn't stuck in the office, closed off from the lovely sunshine.

As she drove the van into the parking lot, she spotted a man wielding a shovel beside one of the graves. He looked elderly and Lucy instantly decided he wouldn't be dangerous to approach, not that she was frightened of doing so anyway. Her appearance invariably disarmed people.

She loved putting herself together in a fun outfit. The Sunday Markets at Port Douglas were always great for crafty stuff. The wooden bead necklaces and bangles she'd bought yesterday, along with the tan leather belt, and sandals that strapped in criss-crosses up her lower legs, looked fabulous with the white broderie anglaise miniskirt and peasant blouse she was wearing today. Her long blond hair was piled up on top of her head to show off the cute dangly wooden earrings, as well. She didn't look like officialdom and that was half the battle in getting people to confide in her.

The elderly man caught sight of her walking towards him, and stopped digging, leaning on the long handle of his shovel as he watched her approach, looking her up and down as most men did, regardless of age. She could now see two large plastic bags of potting soil lying on the ground beside him, and behind them was the top of a rose bush.

'Well, you're a pretty sight for sore eyes, girlie,' he greeted her, his mouth slowly curving into a wistful little smile. 'Visiting a loved one?'

'Yes, I always visit my mother when I come out here,' Lucy said with her own wistful smile. The man's face was so lined and dotted with age spots she guessed he was about eighty, but his body had a spry wiriness that undoubtedly came from keeping himself active.

'Your mother, eh? Must have died young,' he remarked.

Lucy nodded. 'She was only thirty-eight.' Ten years older than Lucy was now—a fact that lay constantly in the back of her mind, urging her to pack as much into her life as she could.

'What took her?' the man asked sympathetically.

'Cancer.'

'Ah, that's a hard death.' He shook his head sadly. 'Guess I should be grateful my wife went quickly. Heart gave out. Coming up seventy-five she was. Almost made it to our diamond wedding anniversary.'

'You must have had a happy marriage,' Lucy commented, wondering if it was really true. She had observed that some couples stayed together because they didn't want to face the turmoil of breaking up.

'My Gracie was a wonderful woman.' There was love and longing in his voice. 'Wouldn't have swapped her for anyone. She was the best, the only one for me. I miss her so much....' Tears welled into his eyes.

'I'm sorry,' Lucy said softly, waiting until he'd re-

covered his composure before asking, 'Are you planting that rose for her?'

'Yes,' he answered huskily. 'Gracie loved roses.
Especially this one—Pal Joey—because it has such
a beautiful scent. Not like those hothouse roses they
sell in shops. Here...' he bent down and picked up the
bagged rose bush, pointing out the one yellow rose in
full bloom '...come and smell it.'

She did. The scent was stunningly strong and beautiful. 'Oh, that's lovely!'

'I brought it from our garden. I couldn't let my Gracie lie here without some part of our garden, and this
was her favourite rose.'

'Well, Mr...?' Lucy raised her eyebrows quizzically,
needing his name.

'Robson. Ian Robson.'

'Lucy Flippence,' she responded. 'I have to tell you
I'm from cemetery administration, Mr Robson. Someone reported you digging at a grave and I was sent out
to investigate, but I can see there's no harm being done.'

He frowned over any possible interference to his
plan. 'Only want to plant the rose.'

'I know,' Lucy soothed. 'What you're doing is fine
with me. You'll tidy up afterwards, won't you? Leave
your wife's grave looking much nicer than it was before, take the empty bags away?'

'Don't you worry, Miss Flippence. I'll not only do
that, but you can count on me tending to this rose bush,
feeding it and pruning it so it will bloom beautifully
for my Gracie.'

Lucy gave him a warm smile. 'I'm sure you will, Mr

Robson. It's been a pleasure meeting you. I'll go visit my mother now.'

'God bless,' he said in parting.

'You, too.'

As she walked on Lucy had no doubt that Ian Robson had been a prince to his Gracie. That kind of devotion could only come out of a true love which lasted a lifetime. However rare that was, it was comforting to know it did happen—could happen for her if she was super, super lucky.

She stopped at her mother's grave, sighing heavily at what Ellie had insisted be printed on the headstone:

Veronica Anne Flippence
Beloved Mother of Elizabeth and Lucy

No 'Beloved Wife of George,' because that would have been a huge lie. As soon as their mother had been diagnosed with terminal cancer their father had deserted them. Not that he would have been any help during those long months of suffering. Every time he'd come home on leave from his mining job in Mount Isa he'd ended up getting drunk and abusive. Better that he had left his daughters to look after their mother, but the desertion certainly demonstrated there was not even common decency in his character—a frog of the worst order.

Ellie had found out he'd had another woman in Mount Isa and was leading a double life—a cheat on top of everything else. Lucy was glad he had dropped out of their lives. She still hated him for not giving her mother the love she had deserved. There'd been no roses in their marriage—none that Lucy could remember.

'It's Ellie's birthday today, Mum,' she said out loud. 'I'm sure you know that. I bought her a gorgeous butterfly blouse and a lovely green skirt to go with it. She's fallen into a dowdy rut and I want to break her out of it. You said for us to always look out for each other, and Ellie does more than her fair share of that, helping me over hurdles I can't leap like everyone else because of my dyslexia. I'm trying to help her to meet a prince. Guys notice colourful people. She has to give herself a chance, don't you think?'

Lucy smiled at what Ellie had told her over the phone this morning—that her long brown hair was cut and dyed auburn. That was a step in the right direction. If her sister would just lighten up a bit, have some fun, show she was enjoying herself… Guys liked that. In fact, they gravitated towards women who emitted a joy in life.

'If you can perform a miracle, Mum, it would be fantastic if two princes showed up for Ellie and me today. Okay? That would be a birthday to remember.' Lucy heaved another big sigh at the improbability of this happening. 'In the meantime, I've got to go and collect some angels' heads so they don't get damaged any more than they are already. Bye now.'

When she reached the memorial garden, she stood aghast at the number of headless angels. The dog must have been a huge German shepherd or Great Dane. It sure had run amok here. She picked up one head, realised how heavy it was, lay it back down and went to bring the van closer to the garden. It took her an hour to load them all up for transport to the stonemason.

Checking the time, she decided that job could wait until after lunch. If she didn't get to Ellie's office before twelve o'clock, her sister might go off somewhere by herself. Lucy could call her, but surprising her was better. What was a birthday without a nice surprise?

Finding a parking space close to the Finn Franchises building was impossible. Lucy ended up two blocks away from the Esplanade, where it was located. She half ran the distance and managed to arrive at Ellie's office just a few minutes after noon. Having paused long enough to catch her breath, she knocked on the door and opened it enough to poke her head around it to check if the room was occupied. Ellie—a brand-new Ellie—sat at a desk.

It put a wide grin on Lucy's face as she asked, 'Okay to come in?'

'Yes.'

Given the affirmative, she literally bounced in, twirling to shut the door behind her, then dancing over to the desk in an ecstasy of delight over the dramatic change in her sister's appearance. 'Ooh...I *love* the hair, Ellie,' she happily enthused, hitching herself onto the edge of the desk for a close look at the new style. 'It's very sexy. Gives you that just-out-of-bed tumbled look and the colour really, really suits you. It complements the clothes I picked out for you brilliantly. I have to say you look absolutely marvellous. Now tell me you *feel* marvellous, too.'

The slightly uncertain expression on her sister's face cracked into a smile. 'I'm glad I made the change.'

Then, typically Ellie, she turned attention away from herself. 'How was your weekend?'

'Oh, so-so.' Lucy waved her hand airily, then pulled a woeful grimace. 'But I've had the most terrible morning.'

She didn't want to relate the frog in the Irish pub episode. No negatives about men today, with Ellie looking so beautiful. Lucy rattled on about the rose planting at the grave and the dog damage in the memorial garden, describing the scene and what she had to do about it, how heavy the angels' heads were....

It was a really good story, yet Ellie was clearly distracted from it, her gaze sliding away, fixing on some point at the other end of the room.

'Angels' heads...' a male voice said in a rich tone of incredulous wonder.

It sent a weird quiver down Lucy's spine. She didn't know if sound vibrations could squeeze her heart, but something did. She whipped her head around, feeling an instant urge to check out the owner of *that voice*.

And there he was—tall, dark and handsome, the perfect image of a storybook prince!

CHAPTER TWO

EVERYTHING IN MICHAEL Finn's mind was blown away by the vision of stunning femininity perched on the edge of Elizabeth's desk. The legs hit him first—long, beautiful legs, glowing with a golden tan, their shapely calves accentuated by straps running up from her sandals. A white frilly skirt ended at midthigh. A white peasant blouse hung off one perfectly rounded shoulder. A mass of shiny blond hair was piled loosely on top of her head, some curly strands of it escaping whatever pins she'd used.

Her face was turned towards Elizabeth, but there was certainly nothing jarring about its profile, and a fascinating dimple kept flashing in her cheek as she talked, her voice lilting with animation. Arty earrings swayed against her lovely long neck, bangles jingled on her arms as her hands waved around in graceful gestures, and the story she was telling was as mesmerising as the rest of her.

'Angels' heads…?'

The words spilled from his mouth, escaping from the bubble of incredulity bouncing around his brain. He could hardly believe the heart-grabbing impact she was having on him, and her mention of angels added to the sense of an out-of-this-world encounter.

He was used to sizing women up before deciding if he was willing to put the time into having an ongoing relationship with them. He never rushed into a decision because it was so tedious breaking off the connection when he found it didn't suit him. But the *rush* he was feeling with this woman in his sights triggered a wildly rampant compulsion to forge a connection with her right now before she could disappear on him.

Her head turned towards him. Surprise lit her lovely face, her eyes widening as she stared at him—big brown eyes with amber sparkles in them. Shiny coral lipstick highlighted her lush, sexy mouth as it dropped open to emit a breathy, 'Wow!'

It echoed the *wow* zinging around Michael's mind, and he felt himself stirring as her gaze flicked over him, uninhibitedly checking out his physique. Her open interest in him was like an electric charge. He had an erection in no time flat—which had never happened to him at a first meeting with any woman, not even when he was a randy teenager. At thirty-five, this was a totally new experience and a slightly discomforting one. He prided himself on always being in control.

'Are you Ellie's boss?' she asked, her head tilting as though her mind was racing through possibilities between them.

Ellie...? It took him several moments to wrench his thoughts away from the rage of desire burning through his bloodstream, and connect the name to Elizabeth. 'Yes. Yes, I am,' he finally managed to answer. 'And you are?'

'Lucy Flippence. Ellie's sister. I work in cemetery administration, so I often have to deal with angels,' she said, as though needing to explain to him that she wasn't off the planet, but an ordinary human being with a proper job to do.

'I see,' he said, thinking she wasn't the least bit ordinary.

She hopped off her perch on the desk and crossed the floor to him with her hand extended. Curvy hips swayed. Perky breasts poked out at him. She was tall, slim and so exquisitely female that all his male hormones were buzzing.

'Pleased to meet you.' Her smile was entrancing. 'Okay if I call you Michael?'

'Delighted.' He took her hand and held on to it, the soft warmth of it making his skin tingle with excitement at this first physical contact.

He suddenly registered movement at his side, reminding him he'd just come out of a serious business meeting with his brother. Harry was stepping up, expecting an introduction. Was he feeling the same impact, wanting Lucy's attention turned to him, centred on him? Michael fiercely hoped not. He didn't want to fight his brother over a woman, but he would with this one. A highly primitive sense of possession was swirling through his gut.

His eyes telegraphed hard warning-off signals at Harry as he turned to make the introduction. This was no-go territory. Don't make a contest of it. They had always respected each other's interest in their targeted women, but Lucy had to be a magnet for any man. Even as he said, 'This is my brother, Harry,' Michael willed him to accept he had first claim.

His heart swelled with satisfaction when Lucy left her hand in his grasp and simply raised her other hand in a blithe greeting, tossing a 'Hi, Harry!' at his brother in a kind of bubbly dismissal.

'Charmed,' Harry purred at her.

The flirtatious tone didn't raise so much as a flicker of response. Her gaze instantly connected to Michael's again, the warm brown eyes appealing for understanding and, to his mind, much more than that to come from him. He felt her reaching out, wondering, wanting....

'I don't know if you know, but it's Ellie's birthday today,' she said, 'and I thought I'd treat her to a really nice lunch somewhere. You won't mind if I take her off and she's a bit late back, will you, Michael?'

Lunch...*yes,* he thought exultantly. He couldn't wait to have more of this enchanting woman.

'Actually, I'd decided to do the same myself,' he quickly informed her. 'Lunch at the Mariners Bar.'

'Oh, wow! The Mariners Bar!' Her eyes sparkled with golden lights. 'What a lovely boss you are to take Ellie there!'

'Why don't you join us? It will be a better celebration of her birthday if you do.'

'I'll come, as well. Make a party of it,' Harry put in, instantly supporting the idea.

Four was better than three, Michael decided. Harry had to know now that Lucy wasn't interested in him, and he could entertain Elizabeth, which took the onus of doing that off him.

'I only booked a table for two,' his PA inserted, pulling them back to arrangements already made.

'No problem. I'm sure the maître d' will make room for us,' he stated, oozing confidence as he smiled at Lucy. 'We'd be delighted to have the pleasure of your company.'

Her smile of delight was turned to her sister. 'Well, a foursome should be more fun, don't you think, Ellie?'

There was a touch of irony in Elizabeth's reply. 'Certainly no awkward silences with you, Lucy.'

She laughed, seeming to sprinkle sunshine at everyone as she happily declared, 'That's settled then. Thank you for asking me, Michael. And it's good of you to join in the party, too, Harry.'

Michael wasn't interested in having a party.

What Harry called his tunnel vision—usually applied only to his work on the franchises—had kicked in with a vengeance on Lucy Flippence. He saw no one but her. His entire focus, physical and mental, was on her. He wanted her completely to himself.

It didn't occur to him that it might not be a good idea to bed his PA's sister.

All he could think of was how to get her there as fast as he could.

CHAPTER THREE

LUCY COULDN'T BELIEVE her luck. The prince liked her, wanted to be with her. And what a prince he was, not only drop-dead gorgeous, but a billionaire to boot! Ellie had said enough about the Finn Franchises for her to know this guy was seriously wealthy, but had never mentioned he was also seriously sexy.

Which gave Lucy pause for thought as they made their way out of the building and across the Esplanade to the boardwalk that ran along the water's edge of the park leading to the marina. Was there something *wrong* with Michael Finn, something that had put Ellie off being attracted to him? Was he a terribly demanding boss? Lucy wasn't keen on *demanding* men. If he had struck himself off Ellie's possibility list, Lucy needed to know why before jumping in the deep end with Michael Finn.

Though it was a beautiful day and her heart was singing. There was no reason not to enjoy this exciting attraction while it was still lovely and shiny. As soon as they paired off on the boardwalk, the two of them in front, Ellie and Harry behind, Michael gave Lucy a smile that tingled right down to her toes.

'Tell me about yourself, Lucy,' he invited. 'How did you come to be in cemetery administration? You look as though you should be a model.'

He had silver-grey eyes—very distinctive, like the rest of him—and she was thrilled that he was interested in her, if only for a little while. Words bubbled out in an effervescent stream. She told him about her experience of modelling—its advantages and disadvantages—then tour guide jobs she'd had, and he laughed at the amusing stories about people who'd made guiding both difficult and hilarious at times. Moving on to her stint in the dance studio, she was prompted to ask, 'Do you dance, Michael? I mean, do you like dancing?'

It was a strike against him if he didn't.

He grinned at her, half singing, 'I've got rhythm... you've got rhythm....'

She laughed in delight.

'Our mother insisted that Harry and I have dancing lessons when we were kids,' he went on. 'Said it was a mandatory social skill and we would enjoy it in the end. We grumbled and groaned at having to miss sport for girlie dancing, but she was right. You could get the same adrenaline rush out of dancing as you can out of sport.'

'A case of mother knows best,' Lucy remarked.

He winced ruefully. 'She always did.'

Seeing the change of expression, Lucy softly asked, 'Does that mean your mother is not still with you?'

It drew a quizzical look. 'Don't you recall the plane crash that took both my parents?'

'No. I'm sorry, but...'

'It was all over the newspapers, the media....'

She wasn't about to admit that her dyslexia made

reading newspapers too difficult. 'How long ago was this?'

'Close to ten years.' His frown lifted. 'Maybe you were too young to take much notice. How old are you, Lucy?'

'Twenty-eight. And just over ten years ago my mother died of cancer. I didn't take much notice of anything for a while, Michael.'

'Ah…understandable.'

His face relaxed into a smile again and Lucy was highly relieved that a sympathetic bond had been established. She pushed it further, saying, 'I don't have a father, either. He deserted us before Mum died. It's just me and Ellie now.'

'Do you live together?'

'Yes. We share an apartment. Ellie is a wonderful sister.'

The voice of her wonderful sister shattered the lovely build-up of understanding. It was raised in extreme vexation, crying out, 'That's because you're so annoying!'

Startled, Lucy instantly swung around, anxious that nothing go wrong today. Michael turned, too. Seeing that she'd drawn their attention, Ellie rolled her eyes at her companion and huffed in obvious exasperation before saying, 'It's okay. Harry was just being Harry.'

Guilt swirled around Lucy's mind. Had she inadvertently lumped Ellie on her birthday with a man she didn't like, spoiling the nice lunch her sister had been anticipating with Michael? Being completely star-struck by the storybook prince, Lucy might have been blindly selfish in so quickly agreeing to a foursome, not really consulting Ellie about whether it was okay with her.

'Be nice to Elizabeth, Harry,' Michael chided, 'It's her birthday.'

'I *am* being nice,' he protested.

Ellie didn't lose her temper over nothing, Lucy thought, taking proper stock of Michael's brother. He was a very manly man, his white T-shirt and shorts displaying a lot of firm muscle and smoothly tanned skin. The slightly bent nose stopped him from being classically handsome, but the riot of black curls and the bedroom blue eyes gave him a strong, rather raffish attraction. He exuded a confidence that probably meant he was used to being popular with the opposite sex, but he'd be dead in the water with Ellie if she perceived him as a playboy.

'Try harder,' Michael advised, dismissing the distraction by lightly grasping Lucy's elbow and turning her away with him to continue their stroll together.

She couldn't dismiss it so easily. 'Does Ellie dislike your brother, Michael?' she asked, hating the feeling that this foursome had been a very bad idea.

If it was, she had to break it up, regardless of the miracle meeting with this man. A real prince who was truly, deeply attracted to her would pursue a relationship, anyway. It wasn't fair to Ellie, messing up her birthday with a man she found hard to tolerate. Better for them to dump the men and go off together, though that was tricky with Michael being Ellie's boss.

'I don't think it's a case of *dislike*,' he answered with a slightly wry grimace. 'I've never known anyone to dislike Harry. He's a natural charmer, but he does tend to ruffle Elizabeth's feathers with his flirting.'

There was flirting and *flirting,* Lucy thought, and some of it could get a bit icky.

'Don't worry,' Michael went on. 'He'll behave himself now. I've warned him.'

That made no difference if, deep down, Ellie couldn't abide the man. Lucy needed to have a private word with her, suss out the situation to her satisfaction. Impossible right here. They had walked past the park with the children's playgrounds, and were level with the swimming lagoon. Another ten minutes' stroll would bring them to the Mariners Bar, Hopefully, she would get the chance to be alone with Ellie in the cocktail lounge before they went into the dining-room.

In the meantime there was no point in not making the most of Michael's company.

'We'd got up to dancing,' he reminded her with a grin, the grey eyes lit with amused curiosity. 'Modelling, tour guiding, dancing—how did this lead to cemetery administration?'

'Oh, there's a lot of stuff in between,' she said airily. 'I was doing a beautician course while the dancing was paying off. That led to jobs in a department store and two of the holiday resorts up here.' She slanted him a twinkling look. 'I do a great foot massage and pedicure if you ever need one.'

He laughed. 'A woman of many talents.'

She loved the sound of his laugh. It echoed in her ears and seemed to ripple down to her heart, where it tripped her pulse into racing overtime.

What was she going to do if his brother was a frog? *Please don't let him be,* she silently begged. It would ruin this highly promising lunch.

Michael kept asking her questions, seemingly intrigued by her, which was a lovely feeling. Most guys wanted to talk about themselves. He gave her the sense that he'd never met anyone like her before and he couldn't get enough of her, not right now, anyway. Whether that would last... Well, nothing usually did, not on this kind of high, but Lucy couldn't help revelling in it.

Of course, he wouldn't be intrigued by her at all if he knew the truth—that she didn't just flit from one job to another because she was attracted to something new and different. More times than not she ran into an unavoidable snag because of her dyslexia, and she was either let go or moved on before she had to suffer the humiliation of being found wanting again. Her disability was a curse she had to live with, but she was determined to enjoy the good times in between being stumped by it and having to pick herself up and try something else.

Right now the promise of having a very good time with Michael Finn was thrilling her to bits, though she still had to check with Ellie that what was happening was okay with her. She wanted her sister to have a happy birthday. Men came and went in Lucy's life. Ellie was the only person she could count on to always be there for her.

They'd passed the yacht club and were on the path to the cocktail bar adjoining the restaurant when Harry called out to them. 'Hey, Mickey! I'll buy the girls cocktails while you see the maître d' about our table.'

Mickey? Mickey Finn. Lucy rolled her eyes. That was such *boy stuff!* Maybe Harry was simply an overgrown boy, irritating Ellie with his silly immaturity.

'Okay.' Michael tossed back the response, apparently accustomed to being called Mickey by his brother, and not minding it.

Whatever… The arrangement between them would give her some time alone with Ellie in the cocktail bar—time enough to check if the current scenario sucked for her sister.

Michael left them at the bar, striding swiftly into the restaurant to speak to the maître d'. Harry led them to a set of two-seater lounges with a low table in between, and saw them settled facing each other.

'Now let me select cocktails for you both,' he said, the vivid blue eyes twinkling confidence in his choices. 'A margarita for you, Elizabeth.'

It surprised her. 'Why that one?'

He grinned. 'Because you're the salt of the earth and I revere you for it.'

She rolled her eyes at his linking her character to the salt-encrusted rim of the glass that was always used for a margarita cocktail.

Though it was clever, Lucy thought, openly conceding, 'You're right on both counts. Ellie loves margaritas and she *is* the salt of the earth. I don't know what I'd do without her. She's always been my anchor.'

'An anchor,' Harry repeated musingly. 'I think that's what's been missing from my life.'

'An anchor would only weigh you down, Harry,' Ellie put in drily. 'It would feel like an albatross around your neck.'

'Some chains I wouldn't mind wearing.'

'Try gold.'

He laughed.

This quick banter between them gave Lucy pause for speculation. 'Do you two always spar like this?' she asked.

'Sparks invariably fly,' Harry claimed.

Ellie gave him an arch look. 'I would have to admit that being with Harry is somewhat invigorating.'

Lucy laughed and clapped her hands. They were playing a game, scoring points off each other. It wasn't bad at all. 'Oh, I love it! What a great lunch we'll all have together!' She cocked her head at the man who was certainly ruffling Ellie's feathers, but quite possibly in a way her sister found exciting under her surface pretence of indifference. 'What cocktail will you choose for me?'

'For the sunshine girl…a pina colada.'

She clapped her hands again. 'Well done, Harry. That's *my* favourite.'

'At your service.' He twirled his hand in a salute to them both and headed off to the bar.

A charmer, Michael had said, and Lucy could now see how it was. Ellie was attracted to Harry but she didn't trust his charm, maybe thinking he was a bit too slick with it. She should just ride with it, enjoy it, let her hair down and not care where it led.

Lucy leaned forward to press this advice on her sister. 'He's just what you need, Ellie. Loads of fun. You've been carrying responsibility for so long, it's well past time you let loose and had a wild flutter for once. Be a butterfly instead of a worker bee.'

An ironic little smile tilted Ellie's mouth as she drawled, 'I might just do that.'

'Go for it,' Lucy urged, excited by the possibility that

both the brothers could be princes. 'I'm going for Michael. He's an absolute dreamboat. I'm so glad I wasn't held up any longer at the cemetery. I might have missed out on meeting him. Why didn't you tell me your boss was gorgeous?'

'I've always thought him a bit cold.'

Lucy threw up her hands at her sister's lack of discernment. 'Believe me. The guy is hot! He makes me sizzle.'

Ellie shrugged. 'I guess it's a matter of chemistry. Harry is the hot one for me.'

Chemistry...yes! That explained everything. There was nothing *wrong* with Michael. Quite simply, there was no chemistry between him and Ellie, and no one could make that happen. It either did or it didn't. Lucy had met some really nice guys in her time, but there'd been no point in dating them. They just didn't do it for her.

She sat back contentedly, the narky questions that had been niggling at her making a complete exit, leaving her free to fall in love again.

She grinned at Ellie. 'Brothers and sisters...wouldn't it be great if we ended up together, all happy families?'

It was a lovely fantasy! Totally off the wall, because Lucy knew she wasn't good enough to hold on to a man of Michael Finn's calibre. Today was hers. Probably tonight. Maybe she would have him for a week or two if she could manage not to be found wanting by him.

'I think that's a huge leap into the future,' her sister commented, rolling her eyes at Lucy. 'Let's just take one day at a time.'

Sensible, as always.

And completely right, as always.

But Lucy was flying high and didn't want to be brought down to earth.

That could happen tomorrow or the next day or the next....

Today she was over the moon and wanted to stay there.

CHAPTER FOUR

WHILE LUCY DIDN'T believe in big dreams for herself, she saw no reason for Ellie not to have them. Her sister was brilliant at everything. No one could find fault with her. However, her personal life certainly needed brightening, and Harry Finn looked like the right man to do it if she'd simply fling the door open and let him in.

'You're always so sensible, Ellie,' Lucy chided, wanting her to lighten up and take a few risks for once.

'Which is something I value very highly in your sister,' Michael said warmly, picking up on her words as he appeared beside them and seated himself next to her on the lounge.

'Oh, I do, too,' she quickly agreed, liking him all the more for appreciating this quality in his PA. She bestowed a brilliant smile of approval on him as she added, 'But I also want Ellie to have fun.'

'Which is where I come in,' Harry said, also catching her words as he came back. His eyes danced with wicked mischief as he gazed at Ellie. 'Starting with cocktails. The bartender will bring them over. Here are the peanuts and pretzels.'

He placed a bowl of them on the table and settled

himself beside her, throwing her a challenging look that mocked any resistance to having fun with him. She flicked him a sizzling glance in return.

Definitely something hot going on between them, Lucy thought, and gave Harry an approving smile as she asked, 'What cocktail did you order for Michael?'

'A Manhattan. Mickey is highly civilised. He actually forgets about sunshine until it sparkles over him.'

Lucy laughed at the teasing reference to herself as the sunshine girl. 'And for yourself?'

'Ah, the open sea is my business. I'm a salty man, so I share Elizabeth's taste for margaritas.'

'The open sea?' Lucy queried.

'Harry looks after the tourist side of Finn's Fisheries,' Michael answered. 'I take care of buying in the stock for all our franchises.'

'Ah!' She nodded, understanding why Harry was dressed the way he was.

She knew Finn's Fisheries was a huge franchise with outlets all around Australia. They not only stocked every possible piece of fishing gear, a lot of it imported, but the kind of clothing that went with it: wetsuits, swimming costumes, shorts, T-shirts, hats. The range of merchandise was fantastic and Ellie had told her Michael dealt with all that.

She knew about the tourist side, too, having been a tour guide herself. There were Finn dive boats offering adventures around the Great Barrier Reef, Finn deep sea fishing yachts for hire, and for the really rich, the exclusive getaway resort of Finn Island, where she'd never been but would love to go.

Harry couldn't be too much of a playboy if he was

responsible for keeping these enterprises running successfully. She noticed that his white T-shirt with the
tropical fish had the emblem of Finn Island printed
below his left shoulder, and wondered if he'd come from
there this morning. Maybe if she and Michael hit it off
really well, he would take her to the glamorous getaway.

Lucy decided she could not have wished for a more
exciting situation—Ellie and Harry, she and Michael.
The conversation over cocktails zipped with good humour. Ellie drank a second margarita, definitely loos-
ening up, hopefully throwing caution to the winds. A
thirtieth birthday was not a time to be overly sensible.

Lucy wanted her sister to have the best possible day.

Which led to making *the mistake!*

They were handed menus as soon as they were seated
in the dining-room, and instead of waiting for the others to start talking about the dishes listed, as she usually did, the fact that they were at a top-line restaurant
gave her the confidence to say, 'I bet I know what you're
going to order, Ellie.'

Her sister raised her eyebrows. 'What?'

Lucy grinned at her. 'The chilli mud crab.' It was
her absolute favourite dish.

'Actually, I can't see that on the menu,' Michael said,
glancing quizzically at her.

'Oh, I didn't really look. I just assumed,' she replied quickly, silently cursing herself for being an im-
pulsive idiot.

Revealing her disability to a man she wanted to im-
press—a man as smart as Michael Finn—would make
him lose interest in no time flat, and she would shrivel
up inside if he got that look on his face—the look that

saw her as defective. Hiding her dyslexia was always the best course. Now she had to cover up the stupid mistake.

Pretending to study the menu properly, she asked, 'What have you decided on, Michael?'

'The steak.'

'How about sharing a seafood platter for two with me, Elizabeth?' Harry said, leaning closer to point out the platter's contents on the menu. 'You get crab on it, as well as all the other goodies, and we can nibble away on everything as we please.'

Lucy instantly warmed to him even more—a sweet man, not only caring about her sister's pleasure, but also taking the meal selection heat off herself.

'Harry will eat the lion's share,' Michael warned.

Harry instantly raised a hand for solemn vowing. 'I swear I'll give you first choice of each titbit.'

'Okay, that's a done deal,' she said, closing the menu and slanting him a smile.

'Sealed with a kiss,' he said, bright blue eyes twinkling wickedly as he leaned closer still and pecked her on the cheek.

'You can keep that mouth of yours for eating, Harry,' she snapped, probably on the principle of give him an inch and he'd take a mile.

He grinned. 'Elizabeth, I live for the day when I'll eat you all up.'

'That'll be doomsday.'

'With the gates of heaven opening for me,' Harry retorted, his grin widening.

Lucy couldn't help laughing.

Ellie heaved a long-suffering sigh and shook her head at him. 'You are incorrigible.'

'A man has to do what a man has to do,' he archly declared, sending Lucy off into more peals of laughter.

He *was* fun. And totally irrepressible. She suspected that Ellie was holding out against him because she got a kick out of the sparring, as well as not wanting him to think she was an easy catch.

However, their selection of a seafood platter for two didn't help Lucy with choices. She would have to order the same as Michael, which was okay. The steak should be very good here.

Michael was amused by Harry's determined assault on Elizabeth's defences, amused by her determined resistance to his charm, too. Most women would be lapping it up. His brother was going to have to work hard to win this one over, but the battle served to keep them occupied with each other, leaving him free to pursue the connection with Lucy.

He'd been quite stunned when Elizabeth had turned up at work this morning wearing the gorgeous butterfly blouse—totally atypical of her usual style in clothes. A birthday gift from her sister, she'd said—a sister who was as different from her as chalk and cheese. She was so right about that. He could see Elizabeth as a schoolma'm. Lucy promised to be a delicious array of exotic cheeses, and tasting all of it had already become a must-do in his life.

And despite her choice of *white* clothes today—very sexy white clothes—she was definitely the butterfly, flitting from job to job as though they all had some sweet nectar for her, tasting and moving on, clearly enjoying everything that life could offer her, wanting a whole range of experiences.

Including him.

Saw him, liked him, wanted him.

His head was still spinning with the excitement of her uninhibited response to their meeting. No games, no pretence, no guard up—just lovely open Lucy letting him know she found him as sexy as he found her. It was a struggle not to be in a constant state of arousal.

He thought of Fiona Redman, his most recent ex, who'd definitely been into female power games. The convenience of having her as a sexual partner did not stack up against the annoyance of being expected to toe her lines. No woman was ever going to decide for him when he should work and when he shouldn't. The success of Finn Franchises had been top priority in his life ever since his father's untimely death, and that was not about to change any time soon.

However, he would certainly make time to satisfy this sizzling lust for Lucy. It probably wouldn't last long. The sheer novelty of her would wear off and the usual boredom or irritation would set in. He had never come across the magic glue that could make a relationship stick. He always found fault somewhere and that was the end of it. Quite possibly the fault was in him. Whatever… he was going to enjoy this woman as long as she stayed enjoyable.

The waiter returned and took their orders. Lucy chose the steak, too. Wanting to share everything with him? It was absolutely exhilarating being with her, especially when she turned those big brown eyes on him, the golden specks in them glowing with warmth.

'You said dancing lessons interfered with sport, Michael. What did you like playing?' Dimples flashed in her cheeks as she spoke.

He smiled reminiscently. 'Everything in those days—cricket, baseball, tennis, soccer, rugby.'

'Not now?'

'They were mostly schoolboy passions. I still play tennis, but only socially. I have a couple of games of squash during the week to loosen up from too much desk work, and usually a round of golf at the weekend.' She looked sublimely fit, probably from dancing, but out of interest he asked, 'What about you? Any sporting passions?'

'I can play tennis, but like you, only socially. At school I mostly concentrated on athletics.'

He grinned. 'High-jump champion?'

His instant assumption surprised her. 'How did you guess?'

'Long legs. Great shape, too.'

And he couldn't wait to have them wound around him in an intimate lock.

'You're obviously in great shape yourself,' she retorted, her eyes simmering with the same kind of thoughts, driving his excitement metre higher. Then, as though taking a mental back step, she added, 'I also play netball with a group of friends once a week. I always keep up with my girlfriends. Men can come and go, but real friends stay in your life.'

'You don't count any men as real friends?'

'A few gay guys. They're lovely people. Lots of empathy and caring.'

'No straight ones?'

Her dimples deepened as her luscious lips twitched into a provocative little smile. 'Well, sooner or later most straight men turn into frogs.'

'Frogs?' he repeated, needing enlightenment. He'd heard 'empathy and caring' loud and clear but 'frogs'?

Her eyes danced teasingly at him. 'You suddenly turn up in my life and everything about you shouts that you're a prince amongst men.'

A prince. That was a surprisingly sweet stroke to his ego.

Her hands lifted in a helpless gesture. 'But how do I know you won't turn into a frog tomorrow?'

'Ah!' he said, understanding. 'You've been with guys who haven't lived up to their promise.'

She shrugged prettily, the off-the-shoulder sleeve of her peasant blouse sliding lower on her upper arm. 'It happens,' she said in airy dismissal. 'I'm hoping not to be disappointed with you, Michael.'

The seductive challenge sizzled straight to his groin. He was up for it, all right. He wished he could whizz her straight off to bed. How long would this birthday luncheon go on—main course, sweets, coffee? At least another hour and a half. He'd give Elizabeth the rest of the afternoon off, take Lucy to his penthouse apartment. Although...

'Do you have to get back to work this afternoon?' he asked.

'Yes, I do,' she answered ruefully. 'I have to deliver the angels' heads to the stonemason, take the van back to the office, then visit the people who own the burial plot that's been mistakenly used, and hopefully persuade them that one burial plot is as good as another.'

'Tricky job,' he said with a sympathetic wince.

'Not really. It's a matter of getting them to empathise with the bereaved parents who have just laid their daughter to rest—how terrible it would be for them to have her dug up again,' Lucy explained. The caring in her voice moved something in his heart, reminding him of laying his parents to rest, the final closure.

Caring, empathy…he sensed something quite special in this woman. She wasn't just fantastically sexy. There was much more to her. So far it was all good.

'Are you free tonight?' he asked, not wanting to wait any longer to have her to himself.

'Yes.'

Her smile promised an eagerness that matched his for a more intimate encounter. Which made his hard-on even harder.

Fortunately, the waiter showed good timing in arriving with their main course. Their conversation moved to food as they ate their steaks, which were perfectly cooked, asparagus on the side with a touch of Béarnaise sauce, and crunchy roasted potatoes.

Lucy was into cooking, loved experimenting with different combinations of ingredients. Better and better, Michael thought, looking forward to enjoying many meals with her. She had an infectious enthusiasm for life that made her company an absolute delight. He was wondering if she'd ever cooked frogs legs after bidding a frog goodbye when Harry claimed his attention, leaning an elbow on the table and pointing a finger at him.

'Mickey, I have the solution to my problem with the resort.'

The problem that had brought him to the office

this morning—the discovery that the resort manager was feathering his own nest at their expense. Michael frowned over the interruption. He didn't want to talk family business with his brother when he had plans to make with Lucy.

'You have to clear that guy out, Harry,' he said tersely—the same advice he'd given earlier. 'Once you confront him you can't leave him there. The potential for damage…'

'I know, I know. But it's best to confront him with his replacement. We walk in and turf him out. No argument. A done deal.'

Why was he persisting with this discussion here? 'Agreed,' he said impatiently. 'But you don't have a ready replacement yet and the longer he stays—'

'Elizabeth. She's the perfect person for the management job, completely trustworthy, meticulous at checking everything, capable of handling everything you've thrown at her, Mickey.'

That rocked him. Was Harry off his brain, wanting to mix pleasure with business? The way he'd been madly flirting…was he seriously attracted? This didn't feel right.

'Elizabeth is my PA,' Michael stated firmly, giving his brother a steely look.

Harry dug in regardless. 'I'm more in need of her than you are right now. Lend her to me for a month. That will give me time to interview other people.'

'A month…' Michael frowned over the inconvenience to himself. Harry did have a point. He needed a replacement for Sean Cassidy pronto.

'On the other hand, once Elizabeth gets her teeth

into the job, she might want to stay on,' Harry said provocatively.

Michael glowered at him. 'You're not stealing my PA.'

'Her choice, Mickey.' Harry turned to her. 'What do you say, Elizabeth? Will you help me out for a month… stay on the island and get the resort running as it should be run? My about-to-be ex-manager has been cooking the books, skimming off a lot of stuff to line his own pockets. You'll need to do a complete inventory and change the suppliers who've been doing private deals with him. It would be a whole new challenge for you, one that—'

'Now hold on a moment,' Michael growled. 'It's up to me to ask Elizabeth if she'll do it, not you, Harry.' This on-the-spot decision didn't sit well with him, particularly with his brother virtually railroading him into it, yet it was a credible solution to the problem.

'Okay. Ask her.'

Michael heaved an exasperated sigh, disliking the sense of having been pushed into a corner. 'It's true,' he reluctantly conceded. 'You would be helping us out if you'd agree to step in and do what needs to be done at the resort. I have every confidence in your ability to handle the situation. Every confidence in your integrity, too. I hate losing you for a month….'

He grimaced at the prospect. She was his right hand in the office, always understanding and delivering whatever was needed. Gritting his teeth, he muttered, 'I guess someone from the clerical staff can fill in for a while….'

'Andrew. Andrew Cook,' she suggested, which meant she had already decided to go with Harry.

'Too stodgy. No initiative,' Michael said, hating the idea of having to do without her.

'Absolutely reliable in doing whatever task he's set,' she argued.

'I take it that's a yes to coming to the island with me,' Harry noted, grinning from ear to ear.

She shot him a quelling look. 'I'm up for the challenge of fixing the management problems, nothing else, Harry.'

Good! Michael thought. Elizabeth wasn't about to mix business with pleasure. If that was on Harry's mind, as well as solving his predicament, she'd spike his guns and serve him right, given that he'd have to put up with Andrew Cook while she was away.

'That's it then,' he said, resigned to a month of having to spell out everything to his *pro tem* PA.

'A whole month! I'll miss you, Ellie,' Lucy said wistfully.

Ah, yes! A month of Lucy without her sister possibly butting into their relationship, Michael thought, realising and appreciating the one upside of this situation. It could have been tricky having his PA an ever-present watchdog while he bedded her sister. Absolute freedom from that felt good. A month might very well be the limit of this currently hot connection, anyway— everything done and dusted before Elizabeth returned to take up her position with him again.

'The time will pass quickly enough,' she assured Lucy.

The waiter arrived with the sweets they'd ordered when he'd cleared away their main course.

'We need to get moving on this,' Harry muttered as he dug into his chocolate mud cake.

'As soon as possible,' Michael agreed, looking forward to having intimate time with Lucy.

'Today,' Harry decided, checking his watch. 'It's only three o'clock now. We could be over on the island by four-thirty. Have him helicoptered out by six. We leave here when we've finished our sweets, hop on the boat....'

'It is Elizabeth's birthday, Harry,' Michael reminded him. 'She might have other plans for today.'

'No, I'm good to go,' she said.

Great! he thought. No delay to what he wanted.

'What about clothes and toiletries and stuff?' Lucy put in. 'You're going for a month, Ellie.'

'You can pack for her, Lucy,' Harry said decisively. 'Mickey can take you home, wait while you do it, take Elizabeth's bags and arrange their shipping to the island.'

'No problem,' Michael said, smiling at Lucy. 'I'll give you my phone number. Give me a call when you've finished work and I can come by your apartment this evening.'

She'd be there all by herself. Perfect!

Her eyes danced with pleasure as she agreed to the plan, and her smile was full of sensual promise.

Michael decided he didn't care what Harry did with Elizabeth.

Let them sail off into the sunset!

He was going to make hay with the sunshine girl!

CHAPTER FIVE

LUCY WAS NERVOUS. Excited, too. Much more excited than she usually was about having a first date with a new man, which was probably what was making her so nervous. Plus the fact that Michael Finn was a high-flyer and she had never connected with anyone from his level of society. She was definitely out of his league in any social sense, and more than likely he only wanted a sexual fling with her, which she might as well accept right now and not get herself in a twist about it.

Regardless of his intentions, she wanted to be with him, wanted to experience him, so no way was she going to back off at this point. Besides, a Cinderella could win a prince. Miracles could happen. Failing that, if the worst came to the worst, she could write off her time with him as a case of real lust being satisfied. Because while she had certainly fancied other guys in the past—not like this, not nearly as strongly as this—Michael Finn had her in an absolute tizzy of lust.

Just thinking of him, she was squeezing her thighs together, and when she'd been in the shower earlier, running her hands over herself, dying to know how it would feel with his hands caressing her naked body.

Even now as she prepared the Thai salad to go with the prawns she'd bought on the way home, her stomach muscles kept contracting.

He'd be here soon—another ten minutes or so. The apartment was tidy. The table was set. She'd changed into a yellow wraparound dress with a tie belt that could be easily undone, and underneath it she wore her sexiest white lace bra and panties, wickedly intent on knocking his socks off, though he probably wouldn't wear socks. Or shoes. Easily slipped off scuffs, she decided, like hers. She'd deliberately left off jewellery, not wanting it to get in the way. Her only adornment was a frangipani flower she'd picked off the tree in the front yard and stuck in her hair.

She imagined him wearing shorts and an open-necked sports shirt that could be pulled off in a second. Would he have a hairy chest? Not too hairy, she hoped, but having such thick black hair, and obviously loaded with testosterone, he was bound to have some. She couldn't wait to see, to touch. Her fingers were tingling with anticipation.

The doorbell rang.

Her heart started pounding.

Please let him be a prince tonight, she wildly prayed. *Please let him not do or say anything to put me off him. I want this night to be perfect.*

The rush of desire steaming through her made her legs feel weak as she walked to the door and opened it. Her breath caught in her throat at seeing him again— so stunningly handsome, and the silver-grey eyes shining with pleasure at seeing her. She barely managed a husky 'Hi!'

His smile was dazzling. 'I've been looking forward to this moment ever since we parted this afternoon,' he said, the lovely deep tone of his voice sending a thrill through her.

'Me, too,' she said, smiling back. 'Come on in, Michael.'

He was wearing shorts and a sports shirt—navy and red and white, a strong combination that emphasised his alpha maleness. He handed her a bottle of wine as he stepped into the living-room. 'To go with whatever you've planned to feed me.'

She laughed. 'It's only a light meal. It was a very substantial lunch.'

'Perfect!' He matched the word to the glance encompassing her appearance before adding, 'It's a light wine, too.'

A very good one, she thought as she glanced at the label—Oyster Bay Sauvignon Blanc. Almost giddy with excitement, she certainly didn't need alcohol to feel intoxicated, but she asked, 'Do you want to open it now?'

'When we eat,' he said dismissively, taking in her living space. 'This is a wonderfully welcoming room, Lucy. Did you do the decorating?'

It was a fairly standard two-bedroom apartment, one bathroom and an open kitchen combined with the living area, but she was proud of how they had turned it into their home, and Michael's approval of it was especially pleasing. She set the bottle of wine on the kitchen counter so she could use her hands to gesture at various items as she answered him.

'Ellie bought the basic furniture. I added the cushions and the wall posters and the rug in front of the lounge. We wanted it to be a cheerful place to come home to, and with the walls and floor tiles being white, the whole place virtually begged for bright splashes of colour.'

'You've done a brilliant job.' He gave her another dazzling smile, setting off a fountain of joy inside her. 'My mother was great at using colour to please the eye, too.'

Being compared to his mother felt like a huge compliment. Lucy beamed at him. 'I'm glad you like it.'

He shook his head slightly as he moved towards where she stood in front of the kitchen counter, 'There's nothing not to like about you, Lucy.'

The lovely low throb in his voice set her stomach aflutter and her heart leapt into a wild gallop when his hands started sliding around her waist. Her own hands automatically lifted to his shoulders as he drew her closer, gently pressing her lower body to his. The silvery-grey eyes darkened with a storm of feeling, searching hers for a reflection of the same storm.

'I don't want to wait any longer,' he said, the plea edged with urgent demand.

'I don't, either,' she admitted without hesitation, every atom of her body yearning to know all of him.

Her lips were already eagerly parted as he bent his head to kiss her. When his mouth made contact with hers—an incredibly sensual first taste—her head whirled with the sudden roaring of her blood. She moaned softly, deep in her throat, as his tongue slid over hers, sweeping her mouth with acute sensation. The kiss fast became more fiercely demanding, driving her into a wild response. The lust that had been simmering since the first moment of meeting flared into passionate need.

Her hands buried themselves in his hair, fingers raking through the thickness of it, grasping his head possessively. His hands clutched the cheeks of her bottom, scooping her hard against him, pressing her so close his erection furrowed her stomach, exciting her further with his strong arousal. Her whole body started aching for him. Her thighs quivered with the fierce desire to feel him inside her, and the rush of hot wetness between them begged for instant satisfaction.

The gloriously devouring mouth suddenly abandoned hers, breaking away to snatch air in ragged gasps. 'Lucy…' It was a groan of wanting.

'Yes… Yes…let's do it.' The response spilled straight off her tongue.

In a spurt of frenetic energy she pushed herself out of his embrace to lead him into her bedroom. 'Come on,' she urged, untying the belt of her dress, taking off the light garment and tossing it onto the lounge as she passed, turning as she reached the bedroom door, looking back to see how he was responding to her wanton invitation.

He'd spun around and was facing her, but seemed stunned into immobility, an incredulous look in the eyes that were raking her from head to toe. His glittery silver gaze lingered on the white lace panties and bra long enough to make the wetness hotter and turn her nipples into bullets.

'You do want me?' she asked provocatively, wondering if he was more used to leading the action than having a woman doing it.

'Oh, yes! Madly!'

The vehement reply shot a bolt of elation into a gurgle of laughter.

He tore off his shirt and hurled it on top of her discarded dress. He did have hair on his chest—a nest of black curls across the centre of it, arrowing down to where his hands were unfastening his shorts. Fascinated, she watched as he pulled them down and stepped out of his remaining clothes. More black curls framed his manhood, which was magnificently primed for action.

Her insides quaked with anticipation. Nevertheless, she never forgot caution, and didn't this time, either. The urge to step back and touch him was irresistible. She took him in her hand, fingers gently stroking the silky skin of his strong shaft as she lifted her gaze to his, appealing for understanding. 'I need you to wear a condom, Michael.'

'Right!' he said, sucking in air and shaking his head as though trying to clear it, while reaching for his shorts again and extracting a packet, holding it up for her to see. 'I did come prepared.' He raised a quizzical eyebrow. 'You're not on the Pill?'

She slid her other hand up his chest, spreading her fingers into the black curls. 'Yes, I am, but that's not protection from everything.' Her eyes flashed him a look of troubled uncertainty. 'I don't know who you've been with before me, Michael.'

He frowned. 'I assure you I'm clean.'

'I want you to be, but I won't risk my health,' she pleaded.

His mouth twisted into a rueful grimace. 'Fair

enough!' He lifted a hand to her cheek, a sympathetic look in his eyes as he stroked where she usually dimpled. 'You've been with a frog who lied to you?'

She grinned at his pick-up on frogs. 'No. I just believe in being careful.'

He grinned back. 'Okay. I'll see a doctor tomorrow. Get a clearance. Can we do without condoms then?'

She flung her arms around his neck, her eyes dancing with relief and pleasure as she rubbed her body invitingly against his. 'You're looking ahead to more of me?'

'Much more,' he assured her in his deep-throated voice.

She lifted herself up on tiptoes and kissed him, deliriously happy that he had so readily accepted her conditions, and he didn't see her as a one-night stand.

He instantly took the initiative from her, claiming her mouth with wildly erotic passion, clamping her body to his, driving up the urgency of the desire churning through both of them. He broke the raging intimacy of their kissing long enough to command action. 'Put your feet on top of mine, Lucy.'

She did and he walked her backwards, keeping her locked to him, the movement making her acutely aware of the hard muscular tension in his thighs, in his entire body. Her breasts were brushing the broad hot wall of his chest, tingling with excitement. Her skin felt electric, buzzing with sensory overload. She couldn't wait to be completely naked, too, feeling all of his maleness everywhere.

As soon as he'd turned into her bedroom, one of his hands slid to her bra clip and unfastened it. Impatient for all barriers to be gone, she unwound her arms from his neck and stepped off his feet, quickly pushing the straps from her shoulders, flinging the bra away, grabbing the top of her lace panties and pulling them down enough to lift her legs out of them.

Michael was wasting no time, either, tearing open the packet of condoms, sheathing himself. She straightened up and for one sizzling moment they looked at each other, revelling in the sight of their sexuality completely open to view. He was perfect, Lucy thought, absolutely perfect, and the glittering desire in his eyes told her she was just as excitingly perfect to him.

He startled her by suddenly swooping and lifting her off her feet, crushing her to his chest. It was a smallish room. The bed was close by, a couple steps away.

'You bring out the caveman in me,' he said gruffly.

She laughed, bubbling over with elation at the possessiveness of his action. When he carried her onto the bed, the same streak of possessiveness swept through her as she wound her legs around his hips in aggressive ownership.

Take me, take me. The words were pounding through her mind, the fierce need to take *him* thrumming through her whole body. She was open to him, dying for him, and he didn't keep her waiting, plunging inside her so fast she gasped at the glorious sensation of the aching emptiness being totally filled, powerfully filled.

She clutched him to her, wanting to hold him there, wanting to hold on to this awesome moment, live her awareness of it to the full. 'Michael…' She breathed his name—the man who lived this moment with her.

'Open your eyes, Lucy,' he commanded.

She hadn't realised she'd closed them, keeping the

high mountain of feeling to herself. But yes, she wanted to share it with him, have him share what he was feeling with her. She opened her eyes wide and caught the fierce intensity in his—the need to know, the desire to take all that she was.

'Keep them open.'

She did, watching him watch her as he began a rhythm of retreat and thrust that slowly escalated to a faster and faster beat, on and on until she was arching, bucking, writhing with the pleasure of it, the excitement, the exquisite tension, building, building to a crescendo of almost agony, teetering on the unbearable. She cried out, her eyes wildly demanding release, her hands clawing his back, her feet goading him on in desperate need, her heart seemingly on the point of bursting.

'Yes...' The word hissed from between his teeth and his eyes blazed with sheer animal triumph as he drove himself into her as deeply as he could, and the agony shattered, melting away on wave after wave of ecstasy emanating from the spasms that convulsed around him.

'Yes...' she echoed, with a moan of sweet pleasure, feeling him pulsating, too, his body shuddering in his own explosive release, his chest heaving for breath, and when he collapsed on top of her, it seemed his heart was drumming in sync with hers, a testament to their utter togetherness.

Long may it last, Lucy fiercely willed.

She'd never had a man like Michael Finn in her life.

She wanted what they had right now to go on and on forever.

Of course it wouldn't...couldn't.

Loopy Lucy—which was what the kids at school had called her—was not good enough to hold on to this top-of-the-scale man for long. *Just cherish the moment,* she told herself. *Hug it tight.* Make it a memory she could hold on to. Unless she suffered amnesia or Alzheimer's disease, nothing could take great memories away from her.

They were hers forever.

CHAPTER SIX

Wow!

For a while it was the only word in Michael's mind. He had been conscious enough of his heaviness on top of Lucy to roll onto his side, but he took her with him, ensuring their togetherness continued. She hooked her leg around him, as intent as he was on maintaining their intimate connection. Her incredibly sexy breasts were softly heaving against his chest. Her warm breath was wafting over his throat. Her arms embraced him as though she wanted to stay clamped to him forever.

She was...amazing!

So uninhibited about showing her desire for him, voicing it, moving on it... no woman in his memory had ever been so actively inviting, making him feel he was amazing to her. His heart started thumping again as he recalled her peeling off her yellow dress, revealing the lovely curve of her back, the long glorious legs and her cheeky bottom fringed in white lace. Then stepping back to stroke him...

His mind had been so blown by her he might well have forgotten the condoms if she hadn't brought up the safe sex issue. He was glad that she had. It was best to be careful. They had no history between them. Only today. But there were going to be a lot of tomorrows. He'd get a health clearance as soon as he could, do away with the condoms so there'd be nothing between him and the whole sensual experience of Lucy Flippence.

His PA's sister...

Amazing!

She was certainly the best possible consolation prize for losing Elizabeth to Harry for a month.

When Michael grew too soft for her to hold him in, she sighed and moved her head to look at him, her big brown eyes shiny with pleasure, a smile of contentment curving her mouth. 'That was fantastic, Michael,' she said happily.

'Fantastic!' he agreed, grinning in turn.

'Shall we go and have a shower together?'

'Nothing I'd like better.'

She laughed, disentangling herself from him and rolling off the bed. 'I'll go and turn the taps on. We don't have a mixer in the shower and you have to be almost a rocket scientist to get the temperature right using both taps. I don't want you to get scalded and—' her eyes danced teasingly '—I don't want you to have a cold shower, either.'

She made him laugh. She made him feel happy. He suddenly realised he hadn't felt this happy for a long time. The sunshine girl... He smiled over the aptness of the name as he followed her to the bathroom.

Showering together was another sensual delight, caressing each other with soap, doing what should have been foreplay, except they'd been in too much of a hurry. He loved her breasts, large enough to fill his hands and firm enough to hold their beautiful shape. The areolae were brown, a very distinctive frame for her enticing nipples, which he'd definitely pay more attention to later this evening…though possibly not much later. He was hardening again under Lucy's erotic ministrations.

'Mmm…' she murmured, looking down at him and cocking her head with a considering air. 'Maybe we should do what we have to do first, or we might never get it done.'

'What do we have to do?' he asked, dropping a kiss on her forehead.

'Pack a bag for Ellie. And we could open your bottle of wine and eat what I've prepared.' Lucy met his gaze, eyes twinkling with mischief. 'Not that you look as if you need to build up your strength, Michael, but it might be even better if we wait a bit.'

'Okay.' He didn't mind waiting, knowing what was coming. 'Elizabeth won't need much,' he informed her. 'She'll be wearing the island uniform while she's on duty, the same as Harry had on today—white shorts and T-shirt with the Finn Island emblem. She'll be supplied with those clothes.'

'So, it's toiletries, make-up, underclothes….' Lucy turned off the taps, stepped out of the shower, grabbed a towel for herself and handed him one as she listed the items to be packed. 'Pyjamas, dressing-gown, the gorgeous caftan I bought her for swanning around in.' She grinned at him. 'It will certainly catch Harry's eye.'

'I'm not sure that would be doing your sister a favour.'

The remark earned him a sharp look. 'You think he wouldn't be good for her?'

Michael shook his head. 'I didn't mean that.'

'What then? Ellie is very dear to me. I don't want her hurt.'

He shrugged. 'I simply have the impression she doesn't approve of my brother. The way he flirts...'

'Mmm...probably doesn't trust him yet. I think she was badly let down by a guy about two years ago. Put her right off men. Harry will have his work cut out winning her over, but she is attracted to him. No question.' Lucy wrapped her towel around her, tucking it in above her breasts.

'What about you?' he asked, wrapping his own towel around his waist.

'What about me?'

'How long have you been unattached?'

'Oh, a couple of weeks,' she answered, waving an airy hand as she headed out of the bathroom.

'You weren't devastated by the break up?'

'Not at all. I'd been going off him for some time and I finally called it a day.'

She entered a second bedroom. He followed, watching as she opened a built-in wardrobe and lifted down a medium-size travel bag from the top shelf. 'This should do,' she said, smiling at him as she turned to lay it on the bed, waving at a chair in front of a computer desk. 'Take a seat while I pack.'

He sat, noting that Elizabeth's room was very different from Lucy's—no vivid colours, less random clutter, more orderly, somehow not as endearing in personality. 'Why did you go off him?' he asked, curious about Lucy's dislikes in a man.

She rolled her eyes. 'He was getting to be a control

freak, wanting everything his way. In my book, relationships should be a two-way street. I am not going to be told what to do, what to wear or what to say, and he actually started answering for me when people asked me questions....' She threw up her hands.

'No respect for the person you are,' Michael deduced, liking her stance for individuality.

'How come you're unattached?' She tossed the question at him, returning to the wardrobe to fetch clothes.

'I wasn't available enough for the last woman I was involved with. She thought I should take off from work any time at all, specifically when she wanted me to.'

'Ah!' Lucy grinned at him as she brought an armload of garments to the bag. 'No respect for your position.'

He nodded. 'Altogether too self-centred.'

She shook her head, wryly remarking, 'It starts off good. You think it's going to be great. Then it all goes downhill.' Her eyes sparkled brightly at him. 'Let's make a deal, Michael. I won't try to change you and you won't try to change me. If we don't gel as we are, then we accept that and part with no hard feelings.'

'Sounds good to me.'

He didn't want to change one thing about Lucy Flippence. Her directness and spontaneity were a delight. He imagined her last guy had been the type to want to catch a butterfly, put it in a bottle, poison it and pin it to a board so it could never fly away and attract anyone else's eye. She was well rid of him.

'I'll just grab Ellie's toiletries and make-up from the bathroom and pack them before I add the good stuff. Don't move. I'll be right back,' she instructed.

It was strange being in his PA's bedroom. It actually felt like an intrusion of her private life, which he'd known nothing about until Lucy had enlightened him. He hoped Harry would be careful with Elizabeth, not treat her feelings lightly if he pursued the attraction that Lucy was so sure of.

Maybe a trip over to the island might be a wise move, to check out what was happening between them. In a month's time Michael wanted a fully functional Elizabeth back in the office with him, and that might not be how it would end up if his brother messed with her emotions.

Lucy waltzed back in with her plunder from the bathroom.

'Are you free this coming weekend?' he asked her.

'Free as a bird,' she answered blithely, placing Elizabeth's essentials in the bag.

Or a butterfly, Michael thought, smiling over his image of her. 'We could go over to Finn Island, see how your sister's doing, stay Saturday night and enjoy the facilities ourselves.'

Her face lit with delight and she clapped her hands in excitement at the prospect. 'I'd love that, Michael.'

'I'll call Harry tomorrow, set it up.'

'Wonderful! I know about Finn Island, of course— exclusive getaway, open bar, gourmet food—but I've never been there. Do you go often yourself?' she asked as she returned to the wardrobe to select more clothes.

'No. Harry oversees everything to do with the island.'

'I didn't mean for business.'

'For pleasure?'

'Yes. I imagine it's very romantic.'

Michael laughed. 'With the right companion, yes. It's not such a paradise with the wrong one.'

'Well, I hope it will be paradise for us,' she said, grinning at him while proceeding to load up the bag. 'This should see Ellie through. She can tell me on the weekend if she needs more.' Having zipped it shut, Lucy grinned at him again. 'Now food and wine and fun in the kitchen.'

Michael was happy with that program.

She led him back to the living room, where she whipped away her towel, picked up the yellow dress, put it on—without underclothes—and turned to him as she did up the tie belt, her eyes dancing teasingly. 'This is safer for me while cooking, but you can keep your towel, Michael.'

He did, enjoying the idea that he was as accessible to her touch as she was to his in the wraparound dress. She quickly provided glasses and he opened the bottle of wine, while she removed a prepared salad and a plate of prawns from the refrigerator.

It was fun in the kitchen. Lucy was playful, provocative and positively entrancing. She had a wonderfully expressive face and he loved watching it as she talked and laughed, loved how her dress swished with the sway of her hips and the bodice gaped with each movement of her breasts. She was so delectably female, absolutely adorable and incredibly sexy.

The meal they sat down to was perfect: prawns cooked in a Thai dressing with a touch of ginger and chilli, accompanied by a very tasty salad. Lucy ate with uninhibited relish. Just watching her enjoy the food was erotic. She emitted a joy in life that Michael realised he'd been missing ever since his parents had died.

There'd been pleasures—many of them, from many sources—but this unadulterated sense of joy bubbling over… His mother had been like that, as though every day the sun shone just for her, and life was always beautiful. The gift of happiness, he thought. Lucy had it, too. Maybe he had found the woman he could spend the rest of his life with.

The fanciful thought surprised him. What had it been—about nine hours since he'd met Lucy? She made an incredible impact, but it was far too early to be entertaining any thoughts about a future with her beyond the month he'd given himself. As she'd said herself, it starts off good then it all goes downhill. Right now it was great, but 'downhill' was probably on its way, sooner or later.

After they had cleaned up after their meal they returned to the bedroom, both of them intent on a slower build-up to ultimate intimacy. Michael loved Lucy's total lack of inhibitions, her innate sensuality, the exquisite delicacy of her tantalising caresses. She inspired him to stroke, kiss and taste her all over, revelling in her responses. It was an act of extreme control to hold off taking her until she begged him to do so, intense need making her voice shrill. His own excitement was at fever pitch and their coming together was even more incredibly satisfying than before.

He was conscious of a wildly primitive elation, almost a sense of triumph in bringing her to such a powerful peak of wanting him. She climaxed almost immediately and he exulted in the hot creaminess of her as he drove towards his own climax—a fiercely ecstatic release that left him floating in a sea of joy.

When he finally kissed Lucy goodbye that night, he carried the joy with him. How this relationship would turn out—whether they'd be compatible as a couple or not—he didn't know and didn't care. He was going to take whatever he could of Lucy Flippence until the joy of her ran out.

CHAPTER SEVEN

LUCY WAS ON cloud nine. Michael had wanted to be with her every night this week. Even on Wednesday evening, when she played netball with her friends, he'd come to the gym to watch her in action, and quite happily suffered being introduced to a group of hot, sweaty women. So far he'd been an absolutely perfect lover, showing no froglike tendencies at all. He was charming, considerate, always ready to laugh with her, have fun, and tomorrow he was taking her to Finn Island, which would surely be paradise.

Her heart was pounding with excitement as she walked along the Esplanade, anticipating their date this evening. Michael had to work late and he'd asked her to meet him at Danini's, a very chic Italian restaurant, at eight o'clock for dinner. He'd booked a table, which was just as well, because there was a crowd of people out and about—lots of tourists enjoying the warm weather, visiting the night markets and filling up most of the tables in the pavement section of the many restaurants catering to them.

'Do you want to sit inside or out?' Michael had asked her before making the booking.

'Out,' she'd answered, preferring the evening breeze off the ocean to air-conditioning, and the hustle and bustle of the street to the relative seclusion of an inside dining-room. She enjoyed watching people, and if she had to wait for Michael to arrive, it would pass the time pleasantly.

As it turned out, she didn't have to wait. Although it was five minutes short of eight o'clock when she arrived at Danini's, Michael was already seated at a table.

'You're early,' Lucy declared, greeting him with a happy smile.

'So are you,' he said, returning her smile as he stood to hold out her chair.

She laughed, instantly feeling giddy in his presence. 'I didn't want to miss out on any time together.'

'Nor did I.'

His eyes sparkled with silvery glints, and Lucy's heart was skipping with happiness as she sat down. A pina colada was on the table in front of her. 'Oh, you've bought me my favourite cocktail, too. Thank you, Michael.'

'Your pleasure is my pleasure,' he said in his deep, warm voice, resuming his seat opposite her.

He was a beautiful, beautiful man. A true prince, Lucy thought, thanking her lucky stars that she had met him. This was an experience she could treasure for the rest of her life.

He handed her a menu, which was always a tricky business for her. 'Have you decided already on what you want to order?' she asked.

He nodded. 'The veal scallopini.'

'I'll have the same.'

'What about sweets?'

She grinned at him as she closed the menu. 'I'll watch what's being served at other tables and see what appeals most.'

He laughed and set his menu aside, content to wait for her decision. A waiter arrived very promptly and took their order, leaving them both to settle back comfortably and enjoy each other's company.

'There's a charity ball at the casino next Saturday night,' Michael told her. 'I bought tickets months ago, more to contribute to the charity than with any intent of attending, but we can join a group of my friends if you'd like to come and dance with me.'

'I'd love to dance with you,' she said truthfully, though meeting his high society friends was a bit of a worry. Regardless of that problem, however, the invitation to the ball was proof he was anticipating a second week with her, which was marvellous.

'Then I'll look forward to it,' he said, looking pleased.

Lucy firmly told herself the invitation also proved Michael wasn't worried about how she'd mix with his peers. On the other hand, he was a man, and on the whole, men didn't look for shortcomings in her. It was the women who could get narky if they thought she didn't fit in with them.

Her friends had all raved over Michael. What woman wouldn't? He had everything!

His friends would undoubtedly be running a more critical eye over her.

The ball at the casino would be a test of whether their relationship could stand up in his world.

Lucy hoped she would pass it with flying colours.

Though Michael had to, as well. For him it would be a test of how well he tried to integrate her with his group of friends, whether he would stand by her side as a true prince would if she ran into difficulties, protect her if she needed protecting. It would be lovely to feel secure with him.

There had been no security in her mother's marriage—not emotional or financial or even physical security—and Lucy knew she would never commit herself to any man long-term unless she was confident she would be safe with him in every sense. Not that she was expecting long-term with Michael, just hoping for longer than her relationships with guys usually ran.

Determined to being prepared when meeting his friends, she gave him an inviting smile and said, 'Tell me about the people we'll be with at the ball.'

Happy to oblige, he described one married couple who ran a wedding bureau specialising in the Japanese market, since it was much cheaper to have a wedding in Cairns than in Japan, with the plus factor of a tropical location. Another couple owned a coffee plantation up near Mareeba on the tablelands. A third couple was making big business out of macadamia nuts, mangoes and other exotic fruits. The rest were singles, but all of them successfully established in various fields—smart, wealthy achievers.

Lucy couldn't help thinking none of them would understand her haphazard way of moving from one job to another. She wasn't *driven* to achieve anything because she had always known her dyslexia would get in the way. Enjoying herself with whatever appealed and was available was the best she could do.

'I won't fit in with them, you know,' she warned Michael. 'I'm from a different kind of zoo.'

He looked totally unconcerned, grinning at her as he lifted his cocktail glass in a toast. *'Vive la différence!'*

The tension that had been building up in Lucy eased. Michael was the only one who really counted, and he liked her the way she was.

Their meal arrived, along with a bottle of red wine to go with the veal. The meat was melt-in-your-mouth tender, the mushroom sauce was delicious and the wine, a full-bodied cabernet sauvignon, complemented both perfectly. Lucy's palate was immensely pleasured by it all and she sat back with a contented sigh when she'd finished eating.

As Michael put down his knife and fork, looking equally replete, she felt a strong sense of being watched. Her skin prickling at being the target of some intense focus, she threw a sharp glance around. Passers-by were streaming past the restaurant, none of them paying any attention to her, but the feeling persisted and her gaze was eventually drawn to a table at the adjoining restaurant.

Recognition of the guy from the Irish pub in Port Douglas came as a nasty jolt. He was staring straight at her, and when he caught her eye he lifted a schooner of beer in a half-drunk, mocking manner, a look of leering triumph on his face. He was with a group of men, probably the same ones who had been at the pub.

They'd been fun at first, flirting with her and her girlfriends, inviting them to dance—fun until they'd drunk too much. They were a bunch of good-looking men who were obviously used to getting their own way with women regardless of their behaviour. They'd yelled abuse after Lucy and her friends when they'd walked out on them.

She'd actually felt attracted to the guy staring at her now—Jason…Jason Lester. He had a gym-toned body, wicked blue eyes and a sexy bristle along his jaw, but by the end of the evening the attraction was stone-dead. And he hadn't liked being rejected by her—not one bit.

Her stomach cramped when he pushed his chair back and stood up, his gaze still trained on her. Alarm crawled down her spine. If he was intent on confrontation… She quickly reached out and grabbed Michael's hand, needing his full attention as her eyes transmitted an urgent warning.

'There's trouble coming our way,' she said quickly.

'What?' He frowned, looking past her to spot what she found disturbing. 'You mean Jason Lester?'

'You know him?'

'Played football against him in my teens.'

She hadn't imagined any connection between them and didn't have time to ask Michael whether he'd liked Jason or not, which drove up her tension considerably when the guy arrived at their table.

'Well, well, here's the honey bee again,' he drawled sneeringly, his gaze shifting to Michael, who was rising to his feet, half a head taller than Jason and more broad-shouldered, but apparently not intimidating enough to stop a jeer at him. 'Pulling in bigger bucks with you, Mickey Finn.'

'You're being rude, Jason,' Michael said tersely, his face set in stony challenge as he added, 'inexcusably.'

'Just thought I'd give you a friendly warning, Mickey.

What looks like all sweetness has quite a sting in her tail.'

'I'd prefer to discover that for myself,' he replied coldly. 'Now if you don't mind…'

'But I do mind. I want the honey bee to spell out why she turned her back on me when she's slept with half the men in Cairns.' The blue eyes lasered hers with vicious spite. 'Well, sweetheart?'

Her face flamed at the slur on her character. That he had made such a nasty crack about her in front of Michael goaded her into a wild reply. 'Even a town slut can have standards, Jason Lester, and you don't meet them.'

'After richer pickings, aren't you?' he retorted, and threw a last mocking look at Michael. 'Just so you know what you're playing with, old friend.'

He left.

Lucy sat frozen, watching him saunter off. It totally appalled her that she'd used the term 'town slut' on top of Jason Lester's numbering her ex-lovers as half the men in Cairns, making it sound as if she was actually acknowledging herself as a slut, which she wasn't. Far from it. But Michael could be starting to see her that way—as a gold-digging slut who had drawn him straight into her bedroom on their first night together.

If Jason Lester and Michael had been friends… If Michael believed him, one man to another… She couldn't think past that, couldn't bring herself to look at the prince who might at this very moment be turning into a frog.

Michael slowly unclenched his hands as he watched Jason Lester make a quick retreat back to the safety of a gang of mates seated at a table in the next restaurant. Typical of him to dive in, hit where it hurt, then run for cover. He'd always been a dirty player on the football field, grabbing guys' crotches and squeezing whenever he could. Harry had got him back in one game, delivering a bit of justice.

Certainly there was no friendship fostered between Lester and the Finn family. He hadn't come to this table to do any favours. His only purpose had been to poison the happy flow of a relationship he wanted to destroy out of some malicious sense of envy. Michael *knew* this, but he couldn't stop himself from wondering how much truth there was in the poison.

The honey bee...

It was an apt name for Lucy, flitting along in her free-spirited way and so sweet to be with in every sense.

The burning question was how many men had dipped into her honey? He might have dismissed Lester's snide crack about half the men in Cairns but for Lucy's retort that even a town slut had some standards. It had been an angry retort, hitting back, yet his own experience with Lucy—her easy, uninhibited approach to having sex—suddenly didn't feel so great to him.

This past week he had been obsessed by the pleasure of her, at the cost of his usual complete concentration on work. Even tonight he'd cut short what he should have done in the office, impatient to be with her again. Had she deliberately gone after his balls because of his 'big bucks'? He'd thought that her joy in sex was part and parcel of her nature, but maybe it was all designed to play him, to take him where she wanted him to go, ensnare him into not looking beyond what she gave him. Was he being fooled by this woman?

He glanced sharply at Lucy as he resumed his seat. Her chin was up at a defiant angle. Her face was taut. No smile. Her whole body looked tense. Her gaze was lowered, seemingly fixed on the table next to theirs, where the waiter was serving sweets. Michael didn't think she was considering what to order for herself, but he decided to pretend that she was. A bone-deep pride insisted that Lester not see he had disturbed either of them in the slightest.

Michael reached over and touched her hand to draw her attention back to him. Her head turned slowly, reluctantly, and when she lifted her gaze to his he saw her eyes were anguished.

Because what she was had been revealed…or because it deeply distressed her to have him think anything nasty of her? There was no certain way of telling at this moment, and he wasn't about to sit in judgement with Lester watching.

Michael quickly composed an indulgent smile and nodded to the next table. 'Do you fancy any of the sweets being served over there?'

'What?' she asked in a dazed fashion.

'You said you wanted to see what sweets other people ordered before you decide,' he reminded her.

'Oh!' There was a second of utter disbelief, almost instantly chased away by immense relief. The frozen look on her face cracked into a smile that showered him with a gush of warmth. 'I wasn't really looking at them.'

He squeezed her hand. 'Don't let Lester spoil your appetite. I love the way you appreciate good food.'

The smile wobbled. 'He was so nasty. I thought…'
Her eyes searched Michael's anxiously.

Again he squeezed her hand. 'He's gone, Lucy. We
were enjoying ourselves. Let's wipe him out of our
minds and keep on enjoying ourselves.'

She looked at him wonderingly. 'You can do that?'

'Yes.' It wasn't the absolute truth, but he grinned at
her to lighten the moment and said, 'Though I'm glad
you didn't sleep with him. I have standards, too, and
Lester doesn't meet them.'

'I hate abusive men,' she said fiercely. 'My father was
abusive when he got drunk. It was a huge relief when
he dropped out of our lives.'

Michael frowned, wondering what exactly 'abusive'
entailed, if there was any bad sexual history that might
have led to sluttish behaviour on Lucy's part. 'Do you
mean violent?' he asked cautiously.

Lucy grimaced. 'He did hit Mum occasionally. Most
of the time, though, he'd just get mean and nasty.'

'What about you and your sister?'

She shook her head. 'We learnt early on to stay out
of his way when he got drinking.'

Michael sensed nothing hidden behind her answer
and felt relieved that there'd been no sexual abuse. He
wished Lucy hadn't made that 'slut' remark. It sat un-
easily in his mind, along with Lester's 'bigger bucks'
remark.

'Not a happy household,' he murmured, thinking
how lucky he had been with his parents.

'It was happy when my father was away in Mount
Isa,' she said quickly. 'He lives there full-time now.
He's a miner.'

'I see. He came home to Cairns in between shifts.'

'Yes. And it was always a relief when he left.' She shook her head again. 'Mum should never have married him. She was pregnant with Ellie at the time and more or less got trapped into it. She was on her own up here, having come from a broken home herself—no one to turn to—and she tried so hard to hold it all together. I couldn't have had a better mother, Michael.'

'Well, I'm glad of that,' he said sincerely. 'And I'm sorry your father wasn't what he should have been.'

She eyed him curiously. 'What was your father like?'

'He was great. Both my parents were. Harry and I were brought up in a very happy home.'

She sighed. 'Then you must have only good memories of them.'

'Yes.'

'I guess you'll want to give your children the same kind of happy home.'

There was a faraway look in her eyes, as though she was imagining how it might be in the future. *Whoa!* The warning shot straight into Michael's mind. He might have gone there with her before Lester had fired his bolt of poison, but he didn't want a wife or the mother of his children to have earned the reputation of being a slut.

On the other hand, his gut rebelled against giving Lucy up at this point. He'd never had sex this good, and until Lester's intrusion she had been a delight to be with. Michael still wanted to enjoy this relationship. He wasn't looking for any long-term future with her. He just wanted a continuation of what they'd been sharing all week.

The waiter arrived to clear away their dinner plates,

and diverted Lucy's attention to ordering sweets. The rest of the evening was fun and they finished it off with fantastic sex. Michael was content with that, deciding he would simply enjoy one day at a time with Lucy, take the experience for what it was—complete and utter pleasure. If it was his wealth that made her sparkle for him, he didn't care, as long as she kept sparkling. He liked the sunshine. It relaxed him. It made him feel happy.

CHAPTER EIGHT

FINN ISLAND...

Lucy drank in all she could see of it as Michael steered his motor launch closer to the wharf where Harry was waiting for them. They had entered a large bay edged with a beach of very white sand, partially shaded by masses of palm trees. It was a beautiful sunny day and the water was a glorious glittering turquoise. At the centre of the crescent of sand wide wooden decks led up to the main buildings of the resort. On either side, villas were stepped up on hills that were covered with rainforest.

Paradise, indeed, she thought, except for the snake in it. Last night Michael had urged her to wipe the encounter with Jason Lester out of her mind, and she had tried to do that, relieved that Michael's interest in her had not wavered. But somehow it didn't feel right that he hadn't cared about what had been said. Although she had dreaded a negative reaction from him, it didn't seem natural for there to be no reaction at all. Unless he just wanted the sex to continue, regardless of how many men she had slept with.

She'd told herself not to get in a twist about it if

Michael just wanted a sexual fling with her. But if he now saw her as no better than a slut to be used...or even worse, a slut with an eye on taking a slice of his wealth... Lucy hated that thought.

It had wormed its way into her mind this morning and she couldn't get it out. She *had* slept with most of the men she'd dated for any length of time, though not on the first night. It had been different with Michael. The excitement of connecting with him had been so intense that the idea of holding him off until they knew each other better hadn't even entered her head. She'd done what she'd wanted to do, elated that the desire was so mutual.

And he'd made her feel...*amazing.*

Still did.

As though she was the best thing that had ever happened to him.

He was certainly the best thing that had ever happened to her.

Maybe she was worrying needlessly.

He'd been happy in bed with her last night, happy with her company on the boat this morning, touching her with pleasure in his eyes, holding her, kissing her. She'd revelled in the warmth of his manner towards her. If she could just get rid of this uneasy feeling that underneath it all he might have no respect for her, she would be totally happy with what they were sharing.

Harry helped Michael fasten the motor launch to the wharf and led them to a golf buggy for a quick ride to the administration centre, where Ellie was waiting for them. A track wound through the rainforest and underneath the awesome canopy of foliage formed by the incredibly tall trees were masses of tropical vegetation: giant tree ferns, palms, bamboo, hibiscus, native flowers. Lucy wondered if her sister loved working in this environment, so different to city living. Had she found it more relaxing, or was working with Harry a tense situation, given the very personal element of being attracted to him?

Ellie was not one to let down her hair in a hurry, but Lucy hoped she was letting Harry into her life. Two years of strict spinsterhood needed to be broken. Ellie was too young to give up on men. There was pleasure to be had in relationships, even though the guys might turn into frogs after a while. Lucy decided to insist they all have lunch together. It would give her the opportunity to observe what was happening between Harry and her sister.

They alighted from the buggy at a wide wooden walkway dividing the two main buildings. Michael took her arm, tucking it around his, smiling in pleasure at having her with him. Lucy's heart lurched. He was such a beautiful prince. She desperately wanted to be his princess, though she already knew this relationship would not have that happy ending.

Michael would want a family in his future. He hadn't actually said so last night, but she'd felt it in his head and in his heart, and she wasn't the one who'd be sharing that with him. Nevertheless, she still wanted to feel he loved and respected her.

Harry led them into the manager's office. Lucy beamed at her very clever sister, who rose from behind an imposing desk, looking very much in charge of everything. 'This island is fabulous, Ellie,' she immediately enthused. 'What a great place to work!'

'Tropical paradise,' Ellie replied, smiling as she moved out from behind the desk to greet them.

Lucy slipped her arm free of Michael's to rush forward and give her a hug. 'Are you loving it?' she asked, curious to know everything, especially the situation with Harry.

'Not too much, I hope,' Michael semi-growled in the background.

'It's been quite a change,' Ellie said drily, flicking him a sharply assessing look, probably checking if he was badly put out by her decision to leave him for a month. He hadn't grumbled about it to Lucy, but he probably wouldn't anyway, since their relationship had nothing to do with his work, and he'd be conscious of the fact she and Ellie were sisters.

'A good one, I hope,' Harry interjected, drawing Ellie's attention to him.

'Yes,' she answered with a warm smile, which Lucy took as a very good sign.

'Now, Harry, poaching my PA is not on,' Michael declared.

'Like I said before, Mickey—*her choice,*' he replied with an affable shrug.

'Okay, while you two guys argue over my brilliant sister, I want her to show me her living quarters,' Lucy put in quickly, wanting to get Ellie on her own. 'You can mind the office, can't you, Harry?'

'Go right ahead,' he said agreeably.

'Come on, Ellie,' she urged, nodding to the door at the back of the office. 'Michael said your apartment was right here. I want to see everything. And while I'm at it, may I say you look great in the island uniform?'

Ellie laughed. 'Not as spectacular as you this morning.'

Lucy was wearing cheeky little navy denim shorts with a red-and-purple halter top, big red hoop earrings, red trainers on her feet, and a purple scrunchie holding up her long blond hair in a ponytail. 'Am I over the top?' she asked.

Ellie shook her head. 'You can carry off anything, Lucy.'

'I wish....' she replied with a wry grimace, as Elizabeth ushered her into the apartment and closed the door on the two men in the office.

She hadn't carried off the encounter with Jason Lester with any classy panache, quite possibly adding to his nasty slur on her character with her own wild retort, and she wasn't very confident of carrying off being an appropriate companion for Michael at the ball next Saturday night. Jason's accusation that she had come on to one of the Finn brothers because of his wealth might be suspected by Michael's friends. It could also have tainted *his* opinion of her.

Ellie eyed her quizzically, sensing something was weighing on her sister's mind. 'Is that a general wish or...?'

'Oh, nothing really,' she replied airily, not wanting to unload these highly personal problems on her sister. She focused on examining the living-room of the apartment. It looked bright and cheerful, with colourful tropical prints on the cushions softening all the cane furniture. An adequate kitchenette ran along one wall.

A television and sound system were arranged against another. She gestured around, saying, 'This is lovely, Ellie. Show me the bedroom and bath.'

The very modern bathroom had everything any woman could want, and there was no stinginess in the bedroom, either. The queen-size bed had much more space than the king-size singles they had at home. She couldn't help grinning mischievously at Ellie. 'Have you shared this with Harry yet?'

'Actually, no.' She retaliated with, 'Do you want to tell me what's going on with Michael?'

Lucy threw up her hands. 'Everything is happening! I swear to you, Ellie, I've never been this mad about a guy. I'm in love like you wouldn't believe, and while it's incredibly wonderful, it's also scary, you know?'

'In what way scary?'

Because it meant too much that everything feel right between them—so much it made her terribly conscious of shadows lurking in the wings. She flopped onto the bed, put her hands behind her head and stared at the ceiling, knowing Ellie expected an answer, and finally picking a problem her sister would readily understand.

'Michael is smart. I mean *really* smart, isn't he?'

'Yes.'

'So what happens when he finds out that my brain wasn't wired right and I'm a dummy when it comes to reading and writing? So far I've been winging it, as I usually do, but this is far more intense than it's been with other guys, and he's bound to start noticing I'm a bit weird about some things.' She rolled her head to look directly at Ellie, needing a straight opinion from her. 'You've worked for him for two years. Will it put him off me if I tell him I'm dyslexic?'

Her sister frowned in thought, then slowly shook her head. 'I honestly don't know, Lucy. Does it feel as though he's in love with you?'

'Well, definitely in lust. I can't be sure that's love, but I really want it to be. More than I've wanted anything. I want him to care so much about having me, it won't matter that I'm flawed.'

Ellie sat on the bed beside her and smoothed the worried furrows from her brow. 'It shouldn't matter, if he loves you. And stop thinking of yourself as a dummy, Lucy. You're very smart, and you have so many talents…. Any man would be lucky to have you in his life.'

She heaved a rueful sigh. 'Well, I don't want him to know yet. I couldn't bear it if…' She shot a pleading look at Ellie. 'You haven't told Harry, have you?'

'No. And I won't.'

'I need more time. To give it a chance, you know?' A chance to keep this man as long as she could—to have all the pleasure of him—because it was really going to hurt when she did lose him.

'Yes, I know.'

'I've been running off at the mouth about me. What about you and Harry?'

Ellie shrugged. 'Same thing. More time needed.'

'But you do like him.'

'Yes.'

There was obviously a chance for something really good here for Ellie. Harry couldn't possibly see any bad in her. She was clever and classy and sensible, perfectly suitable to be a wife who could manage any-

thing in the Finn world. Definitely not riff-raff—a tag
Lucy suspected might be attached to herself, since she
drifted aimlessly from job to job, living in the moment
rather than planning ahead, because there was really
nothing to plan for, not with her dyslexia blocking any
way upward.

In contrast, Ellie's path forward had always been
clear. The teachers at school had loved her for being so
bright and studious, and she had certainly been driven
by their family situation to make the most of her capa-
bilities, building a career ever since she'd been at business college. To be so good at everything automatically
commanded respect.

Lucy propped herself on her elbow, looking earnestly
at her far more worthy sister. 'Promise me you won't
go off him if things don't work out between me and
Michael.'

Ellie looked surprised at the request, but it was important to clear away any complications in the current mix. When the relationship with Michael lost its
magic, it shouldn't take the shine off Ellie's connection
to Harry. Lucy didn't want sister loyalty to muddy the
waters. That wasn't fair. The idea of the four of them—
brothers and sisters—ending up together was a wonderful fantasy, but Lucy felt compelled to do a reality
check here and now.

'Harry could be the right guy for you,' she argued.
'Let's face it…he's gorgeous and sexy and wealthy, and
obviously keen to have you in his corner. You could be
great together and I don't want *me* to be the reason for
you not having a future with him. I'd be happy to see

you happy with him, Ellie, regardless of what happens between me and Michael.'

Concern and confusion chased across her sister's face. 'But being so madly in love with Michael, you'll be hurt if he walks away from you.'

And who always stood by and tried to make things better any way she could?

Ellie did.

Being the older sister, she had an overdeveloped sense of responsibility, looking after Lucy when they were kids, stepping in when she was bullied at school for her scatty mind, taking charge of everything when their mother became too ill to manage, getting them through all the traumatic turmoil of her death and setting them up as their own little family unit. Ellie was the rock, the anchor around which Lucy had drifted, the one who made a mission of *being there,* no matter what.

No way was Lucy going to cost her sister a chance with Harry Finn.

'I'll muddle along like I always do,' she insisted. 'I'm good at putting things behind me. I've had a lot of practice at it.' She reached out, took Ellie's hand and squeezed it reassuringly. 'You mustn't worry about me. Go for what you want. You deserve a good life, Ellie.'

'So do you.'

'Well, maybe we'll both achieve it. Who knows? I just want to clear the deck for you and Harry. Now tell me you're okay with that.'

Ellie heaved a deep sigh, obviously wishing the situation wasn't complicated. But it was and there was no point in not facing it. 'I'm okay if you're okay,' she finally said, her hand squeezing back, her eyes holding the steady determination that had seen them through many troubles. 'Whatever happens with either of us, we'll always have each other, Lucy.'

'Absolutely!' she agreed, relieved to have this serious stuff settled between them.

It was time now to set about banishing shadows from both their lives. They were here on this beautiful island and two princes were waiting for them. She grinned at Ellie. 'Now let's go get our men!' She bounced off the bed and twirled around in a happy dance. 'Let's have a fabulous weekend, following our hearts' desire and not thinking about tomorrow.'

She paused in the doorway to the living room to give her often too sensible sister a wise look. 'You never know when something might strike us dead, so we do what we want to do. Right?'

'Right!' Ellie echoed.

Life could be very short.

Since their mother had died, that proven truth had never left Lucy's mind. She had to stop thinking of any kind of future with Michael and just take each day as it came.

Forget the shadows.

Live in the sun.

CHAPTER NINE

MICHAEL KEENLY OBSERVED the to and fro between Harry
and Elizabeth over lunch. She definitely wasn't resist-
ing him anymore. There was no mocking, no sparring,
no challenge being thrown out. Harry didn't tease or
flirt. Her smiles held genuine liking. His smiles seemed
to trumpet happiness.

The writing was on the wall.

Harry was winning.

Though not necessarily to the point of seducing Elizabeth into taking on the manager's job. She and Lucy
had a home together in Cairns and the sisters were close,
having only each other as family. He was fairly sure she
would return to her PA job when the month was up. As
for having an affair with Harry, he thought Elizabeth
would be very level-headed about not expecting too
much from him, since she had always perceived him
as a playboy. It was unlikely that she would end up in
an emotional mess over him. She would be guarded
against that.

He wondered now about his initial impression that
Lucy had no guard up against anything. Accustomed to
being with more sophisticated women, who knew how

to play it cool, he had been bowled over by her apparent openness, her spontaneity, the way she seemed to freely give everything up to him—with no guile at all. It had been so different to all his previous experience of the opposite sex, but was it real or was it the cleverest artifice that could be used on a man?

Michael felt uncomfortably conflicted by this question. He wanted Lucy to be what she seemed to be. Wanted it too much. He wasn't used to feeling this emotionally involved, and he didn't like it, not when she could be playing him. He needed to settle this doubt. Hopefully, Sarah and Jack Pickard might help do that when he took Lucy to their villa for afternoon tea.

The Pickards had been a fixture in his and Harry's lives all through their teens and early manhood, with Sarah being their parents' housekeeper and Jack being the maintenance man on their property. Harry had transferred them to the island to carry out the same roles here when that suddenly empty homestead with too many memories had been sold.

They were good people. Michael was very fond of both of them. Even more importantly, he trusted their instincts. How they reacted—responded—to Lucy would tell him how they viewed her as a person, a view uncoloured by the lust she continually stirred in him.

Lucy loved the restaurant, a huge open room overlooking the swimming pool and spa decks, the beach and the bay, with lush tropical gardens on either side. The tables were well spaced, making everything feel designed for relaxation, with no crush, no hurry, just divine surroundings and divine food and wine.

Best of all, the mood around the table was relaxed, too. Ellie recommended some of the dishes on the menu, making Lucy's choices easy and natural. There was no sign of any tension between the brothers, so Michael couldn't be worrying too much about losing his PA, and there was nothing but positive vibes flowing between Harry and Ellie.

It was a great lunch.

Followed by an even better afternoon.

Michael took her up to what he called a pavilion villa. This was perched on a hillside overlooking another beach, facing west to catch the sunset. It actually had a private infinity pool at the end of its open deck. Inside was just as marvellous—a white cane lounge suite in the sitting area with plump blue-and-white striped cushions, a kitchenette running along one wall leading to a totally luxurious bathroom, also in blue and white and containing a spa bath as well as a shower definitely built for two, plus a range of bath salts and body oils and lotions in exotic containers standing ready for use.

The bedroom was on a mezzanine level—not missing out on the beautiful view— and featured a king-size bed, lots of cupboards along one wall, a luggage stool where their overnight bags had already been placed and bedside tables with lamps held up by seahorses. There were artistic arrangements of shells and pieces of coral from the reef, a wall-hanging of white net holding fish made of mother-of-pearl, and large candles giving out a faint scent of frangipani.

'This is heaven, Michael!' she declared, swinging around with her arms out in an all-encompassing gesture. *And he is what makes it heaven,* she thought. *This man who is so impossibly perfect.*

Maybe it was all too good to be true, but Lucy wasn't about to let that thought spoil this time with him. He laughed at her exuberance, moving up the steps to the mezzanine level, where she already stood in her rush to see everything.

Her eyes gloated over him, the classically handsome face, the glowing olive skin, white, white teeth, the so masculine body shown off by smartly tailored shorts in a blue-and-grey check teamed with a royal blue sports shirt. Just the sight of his strong, muscular calves made her feel weak with desire. And the great big king-size bed was waiting right behind her.

'Can we have a siesta?' she asked huskily.

He grinned, his silvery-grey eyes twinkling wickedly. 'As long as you don't expect to sleep too much.'

Oh, she loved him, loved him, loved him, locking her arms around his neck in ecstatic possession of him as he drew her into his embrace. An idea sprang into her mind—one that would give her wonderfully free access to all of him. 'Maybe I'll make you go to sleep,' she said teasingly. 'Let me give you a massage, Michael. It would be criminal not to use one of those body oils in the bathroom, and afterwards I could wash it all off you in the spa bath.'

'Well, I can't say no to that.'

'You strip off and I'll fetch a bath sheet and the oils.'

She planted a quick kiss on his mouth, then danced away from him, down the steps to the bathroom, eager to get moving on showing him how good a masseuse she was. He was already naked and throwing off the bedcover and decorator cushions when she returned, pausing a moment to ogle his taut, cheeky butt. In the flesh, Michael Finn had to be the sexiest man alive, and excitement zinged through her at the thought of having all his flesh under her hands.

He turned and caught her eyeing him. 'I think I see lecherous intent,' he said laughingly.

'I was simply measuring your muscles,' she retorted with a grin.

'Fair's fair! You strip off while I spread out the bath sheet.'

She handed it to him, put the oil bottles on the bedside table and whipped off her clothes. 'Okay, I'm naked, but no looking. This is about feeling,' she insisted. 'I want you to lie facedown, close your eyes and let me have my way with you.'

'As you wish,' he answered agreeably, doing as he was told.

Lucy tried the oils on her skin first, choosing the one with the more exotic scent. She straddled Michael, taking wicked pleasure in sitting on his sexy butt, and dribbled the oil around his shoulders and down his spine, grinning as he shuddered at the sudden coolness on his skin. 'The heat comes next,' she promised, taking sensual delight in swishing her breasts over his back as she leaned across him to put the bottle back on the table.

'I'm getting a breast massage?' he queried, amusement rumbling through his voice.

'No. I was just indulging myself.'

'Indulge as much as you like.'

She laughed and went to work on his shoulders with her hands, gently kneading his muscles. 'You're a bit tight up here. I guess that comes from working at a desk all day.'

'Mmm...that feels very good,' he murmured appreciatively. 'Where did you learn to do this?'

'Part of the beautician course. It's more for relaxing, though, not remedial stuff.'

'I'm all for relaxing. I can take a lot of it.'

'I'm going to give you the whole works.'

He sighed contentedly. 'I love your work, Lucy.'

Love me.

She willed that to happen as her hands revelled in stroking his firm male flesh, feeling the strength of his muscles, loving every part of his physique as she moved over him in a kind of sensual thrall, rubbing his arms, legs, hands, feet. The oil glistening on his skin made him look like an Olympian athlete. The scent of it grew more and more erotic to her. When she told him to roll over so she could continue the process on his front, her pulse leapt into a gallop at the sight of his fully taut erection.

She couldn't tear her gaze off it as she knelt between his legs and ran her hands over his calves and up his thighs. The urge to bend her head and run her tongue around the tip of the shaft was irresistible. He gasped. His eyes opened into glittering slits. She took him in her mouth and he groaned her name repeatedly.

Yes! she thought in wild elation as she lashed him with her tongue and pumped him with her mouth, excited beyond belief by this rabid possession of his manhood. *He's mine.... He's mine!* she thought as her own body creamed in climax.

He jackknifed up, grabbed her, lifted her, pulling

her forward to fit her over him. She took him inside
her, riding him, fiercely wanting to drive him over the
brink, exploding everything else he cared about into
meaningless atoms so that only she existed for him.
He cried out as release spurted from him in uncontrol-
lable bursts, and she writhed over him in an ecstacy of
triumph. *Mine...!*

He was moaning, tossing his head from side to side.
She leaned forward, held it still and covered his face
with kisses. His arms encircled her, pulling her down
on top of him. She could feel his heart thumping. He
rolled with her locked in his embrace, taking the more
dominant position so he could kiss her as he willed, his
mouth devouring hers in a frenzy of passion, as though
he had to make her *his* now. His and his alone.

Lucy exulted in the sense of feeling secure with him.
She needed this. It might not be absolutely real for always, but it was real enough for now. His desire for her,
this marvellous intimacy, the heart-warming magic of
being together...sheer bliss.

Michael didn't want to think. He just wanted to wallow
in the exquisite pleasure of Lucy Flippence—what she
did to him, what she gave him. Yet it was so much—so
much more than he'd ever expected or received from
any other woman, and it had happened so quickly. Only
a week. He couldn't stop his mind from circling around
the situation, trying to weigh what it meant.

Jason Lester's jibe that she was after bigger bucks
with Michael could be true. She'd said herself that she
belonged in a different zoo to his social circle. Had she
sized him up as a mark worth pulling out all the stops

for? It actually felt like a stab to his heart to even consider it, which was a warning of how deeply she was getting to him.

He hadn't really had any serious relationships—more a series of attractions that wore off for one reason or another. No woman had driven him to the point of obsession as Lucy did. He couldn't get enough of her, despite the doubts that were now jangling through his mind. Even his concentration on work had been affected this past week, and he never allowed anything to interfere with his control of the franchises.

Had something changed in him?

Did Lucy touch some chord of need that had been kept locked up inside him?

Keeping faith with his father's vision had been more important to him than anything else since his parents had died. Harry felt the same way. It was a strong bond between them. They'd poured all their energy into building on the strong business platform their father had established, possibly at the cost of a more natural lifestyle, though surely it had been in their nature to do what they'd done.

Maybe it was all about timing.

They'd succeeded in achieving what they'd set out to achieve.

Now, with Lucy suddenly bursting into his life, making him acutely aware he wanted more on a personal level…it made him feel vulnerable in a way he'd never felt before. Not in control. Knocked askew.

Again he told himself to just ride with what was happening.

It was too good not to.

Eventually the situation would sort itself out. Maybe with Jack and Sarah this afternoon.

Lucy stirred, lifting her head to smile at him, her dimples flashing endearingly. 'I'd better run the spa bath if we're to wash the oil scent off us before our visit to the Pickards.'

Weird that she'd thought of them at the same time as he had. He'd told her about the invitation on the trip out, explaining their connection to the family, and she'd seemed eager to meet them, interested in their life on the island.

'Good thinking,' he approved.

Her eyes sparkled. 'I'll use the watermelon bath crystals. That will clean us up.'

He laughed. She rolled away from him, off the bed, and headed for the bathroom in a provocative prance, swinging her delectable bottom, leaving a broad smile on Michael's face and the thought in his mind that she made him laugh a lot, putting a happy zing in his life in more ways than one.

The sunshine girl...

He enjoyed the challenge of his work, keeping on top of everything, but when he walked out of his office, Lucy's kind of sunshine was precisely what he wanted, what he needed to put his world in balance. Did he really care if it was his wealth that brought him this?

He'd prefer it not to be, but it was an integral part of who he was, which probably made it a factor in all his relationships. Except with his brother. Telling himself not to let it cloud this time with Lucy, he swung himself off the bed, rolled up the bath sheet and went to join her in the bathroom.

The spa bath was another sensual delight. She insisted on soaping him all over, her body sliding around his, then directed him to sit between her legs, his back turned to her while she shampooed his hair and gave him a scalp massage. He ended up horny and they had sex again—fun sex this time, with the bubbles from the bath crystals swirling around them.

Michael could not remember feeling more relaxed when they finally strolled down the hill to visit Jack and Sarah. He wanted them to find no fault in Lucy. He wanted today to stay as perfect as it was with this woman at his side.

Paradise…

CHAPTER TEN

LUCY WAS NERVOUS about meeting the Pickards. Normally she didn't care if people approved of her or not, but from what Michael had told her, Jack and Sarah were almost like a second set of parents to him and Harry. They *counted* in his life, so it really mattered to her that they like her.

It helped that he was holding her hand, giving her a sense of security with him, and surely they would see he was happy with her. That should help, too. And Ellie would have made a good impression on them. Her sister had real class in every way. Not that Lucy was like her. She wasn't. But they were *family*.

The Pickards' villa was positioned on flat land between the gym and the huge maintenance shed that housed the power generator and the desalination plant providing fresh water for the resort. Within easy walking distance of the administration centre, and bigger than the guest villas, it was a permanent home for them.

They were both on the veranda that ran across the front of the villa, probably eager to greet Michael and his companion when they arrived. Eager to look her over, too. Jack appeared to be spraying plants in tubs placed around the edge of the veranda. Sarah was in a rocking chair, flipping through a magazine.

As she caught sight of them, she put the magazine aside and stood up, calling out to Jack that they were coming. He set the spray-can on the veranda railing, took off his gloves and joined her at the top of the steps. They were both short, lean and wiry in physique, with iron-grey curly hair framing fairly weather-beaten faces—obviously active outdoors people. And they were wearing cheerful, welcoming expressions that eased some of Lucy's inner tension.

'It's lovely to see you, Mickey!' Sarah warmly declared.

'Likewise,' he said just as warmly. 'And this is Lucy Flippence, Elizabeth's sister.'

'My, my…you're not at all alike.' The predictable comment came as she grasped the hand Lucy offered.

'No. Ellie is as sharp as a tack and I guess most people would consider me fairy floss.' Lucy tossed off the remark with a self-deprecating smile.

'I always thought there was some magic in fairy floss,' Jack said, grinning at her as he took her hand and shook it.

She laughed, relieved that he accepted her so readily. 'I think this island is magic, and Michael tells me you've both helped to make it so.'

'Oh, we do our bit. We love it here, don't we, Sarah?'

'Yes, we're very lucky,' she agreed.

'I see you've got your roses growing well, Jack,' Michael remarked.

Lucy was surprised. 'Roses? Here?'

Jack's eyes twinkled with pleasure. 'It was a chal-

20% OFF*

with code
THANKSJUL

Visit www.millsandboon.co.uk today to get this exclusive offer!

Ordering online is easy:

- 1000s of stories converted to eBook
- Big savings on titles you may have missed in store

Visit today and enter the code **THANKSJUL** at the checkout today to receive **20% OFF** your next purchase of books and eBooks*. You could be settling down with your favourite authors in no time!

MILLS & BOON

JUL13

lenge, but...' he stepped back, his arm swinging out to gesture to the tubs '...coming into bloom now.'

Lucy spotted a yellow bud just opening up. 'Is that a Pal Joey?'

'Yes, it's one of my favourites,' Sarah answered. 'It has such a lovely scent.'

'I know. It's beautiful. I was at Greenlands Cemetery last Monday and an elderly man was planting a Pal Joey rose bush on his wife's grave. He said he couldn't have his Gracie lie there without her favourite rose.'

Sarah's face softened. 'Oh, how very loving of him!'

'They'd been married almost sixty years. I thought it was wonderful. Do you grow them for Sarah, Jack?'

'For both of us.' He smiled ruefully at his wife. 'But should I have the misfortune of Sarah passing first, I shall certainly plant one on her grave.'

She smiled back. 'You do that, Jack.'

Lucy sighed. 'It's so nice to meet married people who are devoted to one another. There's not enough of it.'

'You can make your own world, Lucy,' Sarah said philosophically. 'And how is it that the cemetery features in yours?'

'It's her job,' Michael put in. 'Lucy is in cemetery administration.'

That startled Sarah. 'Good heavens! Do you like it?'

'So far I do. I haven't been in it for long,' she admitted. 'It gives me plenty of opportunities to visit my mother's grave. She died when I was seventeen, and I like to chat to her, tell her what I'm thinking and feeling. It sort of settles me down when I feel a bit adrift, you know?'

She was running off at the mouth as she always did

when she felt nervous. But Sarah didn't seem to think she was weird or anything, taking her hand again and patting it in a comforting way.

'It's very sad, losing your mother so young,' she said sympathetically.

'Yes, though Ellie is great. She takes charge of everything.'

Sarah nodded. 'I can see how she'd do that. She's handling everything very well here.'

'Don't you weigh in with Harry, Sarah,' Michael quickly interjected. 'Elizabeth is my PA. This situation is only temporary.'

'Not my business,' she assured him, stepping back to wave them forward. 'Come on through. I've set up afternoon tea on the back veranda. It has a view of the beach and sea.'

'Can I help you with anything?' Lucy asked as they were led into a large living area encompassing kitchen, dining room and lounge, all furnished in a very homely way.

'I just have to boil the kettle, dear, but stay with me and chat. You can help take the cake and cookies out when the tea is ready.'

'Please tell me they're your peanut butter cookies,' Michael said with relish.

Sarah laughed. 'Would I bake you any other? Go along with Jack now. We'll be out in a few minutes.'

The two men made their exit via a back door. Sarah switched the kettle on, then turned to Lucy, her hazel eyes bright with interest. 'Your sister told me you met Mickey at the office.'

'Yes, it was Ellie's birthday last Monday and I

dropped in to see her. Harry was there, too, and we all ended up having lunch together.'

'You must have seen more of Mickey this week for him to bring you here.'

Sarah was fishing, but Lucy didn't mind answering. 'Every night! It's been amazing! I feel like I'm in the middle of a fairy tale with him. He's such a prince!'

'He is, isn't he?' she said fondly. 'So is Harry. They're both very special men. Like their parents. They were special, too.'

'Michael said he lost them about the same time I lost my mother.'

Sarah sighed. 'A terrible tragedy. But they'd be very proud of their sons. Very proud.'

Realising that this woman had to know Michael's character through and through, Lucy decided to take the risk of confiding how she felt—the doubts she had about how Michael viewed this relationship, whether it could become really meaningful to him in his mind and heart.

She made an ironic grimace and gestured helplessly. 'The trouble is I'm not sure I can live up to him, Sarah. I mean…I'm more or less a Cinderella in his world. He's asked me to attend a ball with him next Saturday night, and I'm scared stiff that I won't fit in with his friends.'

'Don't be scared, Lucy,' the older woman advised. 'If Mickey wants you with him, he'll look after you. He's very like his father. Intense about anything he sets himself to do, and extremely protective of anyone he cares for.'

But did he really *care* for her? That was the big question.

'Then I should be okay,' Lucy said with a smile, thinking she'd probably dug as far as she could dig.

Sarah smiled back. 'I'm sure you will be, dear.'

The kettle boiled and she filled a large teapot that was patterned with roses. Lucy imagined the cups and saucers set outside would match.

'You *are* lucky, Sarah. There were no roses in my mother's marriage,' she wryly remarked. 'If I ever marry, it will only be to a man who loves me enough to give me roses.'

'Can't wait!' Michael announced from behind them. 'I'm going to snaffle a cookie.'

'We're coming!' Sarah chided.

'Fine! You bring the tea. I'll take the plate of cookies and Lucy can carry the banana cake.'

'How do you know it's a banana cake? It's covered in icing,' Lucy pointed out.

Michael grinned at Sarah, his eyes twinkling with certain knowledge.

'It's banana cake,' she conceded.

'You're a treasure, Sarah.'

'Oh, you and Harry always butter me up to get what you want.' She waved to the plate of cookies. 'Take them. We'll follow you out.'

They settled around a large wooden table on the back veranda, which faced a different bay than the administration centre. 'This beach catches the afternoon sun,' Jack pointed out. 'And, of course, we get the sunset view from here.'

As would the pavilion villa up on the hill, Lucy thought happily.

'You have a gorgeous lot of bougainvillea out here, Jack,' she remarked, gesturing to the brightly coloured profusion of them surrounding the veranda.

'They don't mind the sandy soil and sea air. Easy to grow here,' he explained.

'Did you do that wonderful tropical garden around the restaurant?'

Her curiosity about the development of the resort made for an easy, relaxed conversation over afternoon tea. Jack was proud of his work and Sarah was proud of her husband's ability to turn his hand to anything. Lucy coaxed smiles and laughter out of both of them, which always promoted a happy time and reduced any chance of self-conscious tension taking hold.

Michael sat back and watched her charm Jack and Sarah. She had quite extraordinary people skills, focusing on whoever was talking, picking up on their interests, making them seem just as interesting to her. Her smiles evoked smiles, and her laughter was infectious.

When she asked about how the sea water was turned into fresh, Michael quickly suggested to Jack that he take Lucy down to the maintenance shed and show her the process. It would give him some time alone with Sarah, who was a shrewd judge of character. Her opinion of other women he'd brought here had always been spot on.

Jack was only too pleased to show Lucy anything. He was clearly very taken by her. Most men would be, Michael thought, no matter how old. *The honey bee...* Lester's name for her slid into his mind again and he frowned as Lucy and Jack left the veranda together. Lester had given it a sexual connotation, but Lucy had not been consciously sexy over afternoon tea. She was simply...very appealingly female.

'What's wrong, Mickey?' Sarah asked quietly.

He shook his head. 'Just a problem I have.'

'To do with Lucy?'

'What do you think of her, Sarah?'

'A joy to be with,' she answered with a smile.

'Yes,' he agreed. 'Anything else?'

Sarah mused for a few moments before remarking, 'She's quite different from the other women you've brought over here. More spontaneous, artless...'

'Not a scheming gold-digger?' he pressed.

Sarah looked shocked. 'Not at all! Has she done anything to make you think it?'

'I am a very wealthy man,' he said drily.

'That can be intimidating to a girl like Lucy, Mickey,' she quickly argued. 'It can make her think she's not good enough for you.'

'She's beautiful. She's sexy. She's fun. That's a fairly good trade-off, Sarah.'

'If you have a lot of self-esteem, and I don't think she has,' Sarah replied thoughtfully. 'There's not much ego running around in that girl. She focuses on other people, doesn't want the spotlight turned on herself.'

'Because she's hiding something?' Michael queried, wondering if that was the case.

'I don't know. Her comment about being fairy floss compared to her sister made me think she knew she could never compete with Elizabeth, possibly from an early age. So she conceded all that ground and chose a different path for herself—one that didn't demand more than she felt capable of doing.'

'She is the younger sister. Elizabeth called her ditzy,' Michael recalled.

Sarah shot him an ironic smile. 'That's probably a good cover for feeling inadequate.'

He frowned over that possibility. 'I doubt Lucy feels inadequate. She's held quite an amazing array of jobs—model, beautician, tour guide, dancing teacher, amongst other things. It's as though she's drawn to try anything and everything. She dropped out of school to nurse her mother, who died of cancer, and never went back to complete any formal education—said she had no head for study after that. But I think she manages to do quite well for herself.'

'Where was Elizabeth when her mother was dying?'

'At home. Already at business college, so I imagine Lucy did the bulk of the nursing.'

'While Elizabeth prepared to take on the future.' Sarah nodded in understanding. 'Would you say the sisters are close?'

'Yes. Very different but very close. Lucy called Elizabeth her anchor.'

'When she feels adrift...that's what she said about visiting her mother's grave.' Sarah gave Michael a very direct look. 'You don't have a scheming gold-digger on your hands, Mickey. I'd say if Lucy is hiding anything, it's something she feels very vulnerable about. Be careful how you treat her.' His friend's serious expression cracked into a smile. 'She sees you as a prince.'

Michael grinned at her. 'Until I turn into a frog. According to Lucy, most princes eventually turn into frogs.'

Sarah laughed. 'She is a delight, that girl! In some ways, she's very like your mother. A joy to be with.'

Yes.

It was exactly what had been missing from his life, ever since his mother had died.

That was the chord Lucy struck in him—a much deeper need than the lust she stirred. A need for that emptiness to be filled.

'It's been good talking to you, Sarah,' he said appreciatively.

Someone he could trust.

Someone who would never lie to him.

He needed that, too.

If Lucy was covering up something she didn't want him to know, trying to keep him blinded with her fairy floss, he couldn't really trust her.

What did she feel she had to keep hidden?

The number of men in her past?

Maybe he should have questioned her about that last night. Maybe he should do it now. But remembering the anguish in her eyes after Lester had left them with his poison, Michael didn't want to bring that back and spoil this weekend with her. *Let it ride for a while,* he told himself again. But he wouldn't forget that Lucy could be keeping something from him—something that was important for him to know before this relationship went much further.

CHAPTER ELEVEN

LUCY COULD NOT have wished for a more marvellous time with Michael. The afternoon tea with the Pickards had been relatively stress-free. She had not felt any negative vibes coming from either of them. They were really nice people. Michael had then suggested a game of tennis, which had been great fun, followed by a dip in the infinity pool, drinking champagne as they watched the sunset. A romantic dinner for two on the deck below the restaurant had been a highlight finish to their day, eating superb food to the lapping of waves on the beach, under a star-studded sky.

On Sunday morning they slept in after a long night of making love. The fruit platter in the refrigerator was breakfast enough, since they were having an early lunch with Harry and Ellie before setting off to the mainland. Lucy wanted to see them happy with each other, as happy as she felt with Michael.

It was another beautiful, sunny day and harmony flowed between the two brothers and sisters as they sat in the restaurant, enjoying the fine cuisine. Ellie had mused out loud over the choices for each course, making decisions easy. It caused Lucy to reflect how lucky she was to have a sister who cared about her problems.

All through her school years, Ellie had tried to help her with reading and writing. She'd researched dyslexia on the internet and downloaded programs that might untangle the confusion in Lucy's mind. When they hadn't produced a miracle, she'd spent hours and hours coaching her to learn things off by heart. Without Ellie she would never have passed her driving test, which had allowed her to get jobs that wouldn't have been possible otherwise. Lucy owed her sister a debt she could never repay. It was good to see her eyes twinkling happily at Harry. Ellie deserved a prince.

Again Lucy couldn't help thinking how wonderful it would be if all four of them could end up together. That was a *big* dream—an impossible dream—but she was sailing along in a bubble of bliss, until Ellie dropped her bombshell.

They were sitting over coffee when Michael asked, 'Any prospects for the position of manager here, Harry?'

He shrugged. 'A few résumés have come in. I haven't called for any interviews yet. Elizabeth may want to stay on now that she's on top of the job.'

'Elizabeth is mine!' Michael shot him a vexed look.

'No!' The denial tripped straight out of Ellie's mouth.

Lucy was shocked into staring at her sister, who suddenly looked very serious and determined.

Michael, too, was taken aback. 'Don't tell me Harry has seduced you into staying here.'

'No, I won't be staying here beyond the month he needs to find someone suitable,' she replied quietly and calmly.

'So you'll come back to me,' Michael insisted.

She shook her head. 'I'm sorry, Michael, but I don't want to do that, either.'

'Why not?' he persisted.

'Being here this week has made me realise I want a change. To try something different. I'd appreciate it if you'd take this as my notice.'

He wasn't happy. He glared at his brother. 'Goddammit, Harry! If it wasn't for you—'

'Hey!' Harry held up his hands defensively. 'I'm not getting her, either.'

'Please…' Elizabeth quickly broke in. 'I don't want to cause trouble. I just want to take a different direction with my life.'

'But you're brilliant as my PA,' Michael argued, still annoyed at being put out.

'I'm sorry. You'll just have to find someone else.'

The relaxed atmosphere around the table was completely shattered. Everyone was tense. Lucy could hardly believe Ellie had come to this decision. It was like a rejection of both brothers, and the reason she gave… What direction *did* she want to take from here? Shutting herself off from two great careers made no sense.

'Why not try out Lucy as your PA?' Harry suggested to Michael with an airy wave of his hand. 'She's probably as brilliant as her sister.'

Panic instantly welled up in Lucy. *No, no, no!* screamed through her mind. She wasn't Ellie. She could never be like Ellie. She begged help from her sister with her eyes.

'It's not her kind of thing,' Ellie said firmly.

Michael was not put off, turning to remark quizzically, 'You do work in administration, Lucy.'

'I'm the front person who deals with people, Michael,' she stated, her stomach in absolute turmoil. 'I don't do desk work. I'm good at helping people, understanding what they want, helping them to decide.... There's quite a bit of that in cemetery administration. And I like it,' she added for good measure, pleading for him to drop the issue.

He grimaced in frustration.

She reached out and touched his hand, desperate to restore his good humour with her. 'I'm sorry, but I can't fill Ellie's place.'

The grimace slowly tilted up into a soothing smile. 'I shouldn't have expected it. You are a people person and I like that, Lucy. I wouldn't want to change it.'

Relief poured through her at having crossed this tricky hurdle without having to spell out why she'd be such a hopeless alternative to her sister.

'I hope you'll give me a good reference, Michael,' Ellie said, drawing attention away from Lucy.

He sighed and turned to her. 'It will be in the mail tomorrow. I hate losing you, but I wish you well, Elizabeth.'

It was a fairly graceful acceptance of the situation, but Lucy was extremely sensitive to the fact that the congenial atmosphere around the table was not about to resume. Tension emanated from Harry. It was obvious he didn't like this decision, either.

'Thank you,' Ellie said, nodding to Michael.

Case closed.

Except it wasn't.

Stony glances were being exchanged between the brothers. Frustration simmered from both of them. No one chose to eat any of the petit fours that accompanied coffee. Nothing was going to feel good until Michael and Harry cleared up their differences, which could be done only by leaving them alone together. Apart from resolving that problem, Lucy was also anxious to query Ellie about her reasons for leaving the PA job with Michael.

Had turning thirty hit her hard, triggering this sudden desire for change?

Or did the decision have something to do with foreseeing a bad outcome for the relationship Lucy had entered into with Michael? Ellie might not want to be around him if he let her sister down, and maybe she believed that was going to happen, complete with some horrible emotional fallout. If she was acting on that belief…Lucy inwardly recoiled from the idea. She would hate it if anything she did mucked up her sister's career.

As soon as Ellie had finished her cappuccino, Lucy pushed back her chair and rose to her feet. 'I'm off to the ladies' room. Will you come with me, Ellie?'

'Of course,' she said, immediately rising to join her.

The moment they were closeted away, Lucy confronted her, determined to learn the truth. 'Why are you leaving your great job with Michael? He's not happy about it.'

Ellie shook her head. 'It's not my mission in life to keep Michael happy,' she said drily.

'But you always said you loved that job.'

'I did, but it's high pressure, Lucy. I didn't realise how much it demanded of me until I came out here.

I don't want to be constantly on my toes anymore. I want to look for something else—more relaxed, less stressful.'

Was this the truth? Ellie had always been ambitious, and walking away from such a top-level position seemed like a complete turnaround from achieving what she'd aimed for. On the other hand, Lucy knew nothing of high pressure jobs, never having had one, so Ellie might actually need to give it up and move on.

'Then it's not because of me and him?' Lucy asked worriedly, wanting to believe this decision was as straightforward as her sister made out.

'No,' she replied, her eye contact remaining absolutely steady as she laid out what she thought. 'I'm sorry Michael is unhappy about it, but I don't think he'll take it out on you, Lucy. If he does, he's not the man for you.'

Lucy hadn't got that far in her own thinking. Her main concern had revolved around Ellie sacrificing her job out of some sense of protective loyalty. If there were personal repercussions from Michael because of his frustration over the situation...well, that simply wasn't acceptable. He would not be the man for her. It would be frog territory. Lucy was not so blindly in love that she couldn't see that. This was a test he would have to pass or there was not even a small future for them.

She heaved a sigh to relieve the tightness in her chest, gave her sister a quick hug, then looked her directly in the eye. 'You're right. Okay. It's completely fair for you to look for something else. He's just got to lump being put out by it.'

'You can play nurse and soothe his frustration,' Ellie said with a smile.

Lucy laughed, more in the grip of hysteria than from any amusement. She desperately didn't want things to start going wrong between her and Michael, but if they did, she had to be as sensible as Ellie. However seductive a fairy tale fantasy was, in the end there was no escaping from reality.

Michael couldn't recall ever being at serious odds with his brother, but he was right now. He'd lent Elizabeth to him to facilitate the quick removal of a crooked manager. He could tolerate not having her on hand for a month, but losing her altogether had not been on the table.

Just one week over here and she was handing in her resignation as his PA. He didn't buy her reason for leaving him. Something had happened and that *something* had to do with Harry. Michael waited until the two sisters had closed themselves in the ladies' room, safely out of earshot, and unleashed his anger.

'This is bloody nonsense!' he hissed at Harry. 'Elizabeth never showed any dissatisfaction with her work situation. Whatever I threw at her, she ate up, and came back for more. And I paid her what she was worth. She's completely on top of her job. Why the hell would she want to take a different direction? The only thing that makes sense is you've thrown a spanner in the works, Harry.'

'If she wants a different direction, why isn't she staying on here?' he retaliated. 'She's on top of this job, too. It's not me pulling the strings, Mickey.'

'Then what is it?' he demanded testily.

Harry eyed him grimly. 'I'd say it's Lucy.'

'That's nonsense, too! Lucy was just as shocked as I was at Elizabeth's resignation.'

'Wake up, Mickey!' Sheer exasperation laced Harry's voice. 'You're having it off with your PA's younger sister—a sister she's more or less been a mother to after their own mother died. From the moment you took up with Lucy, Elizabeth's resignation has probably been on the drawing board. Seeing how it is for her sister this weekend undoubtedly clinched it.'

'What do you mean?'

Harry rolled his eyes. 'Even to me it's obvious that Lucy's head over heels in love with you. Elizabeth would be well aware that your relationships have never lasted long. You might end up hurting her sister very badly.'

'And I might not!' Michael retorted heatedly. 'I might want to keep this relationship.'

Harry shrugged. 'Whatever… But you introduced a personal element that wasn't there before.'

'What about you? Don't tell me you haven't got very personal with Elizabeth this week.'

'Which is probably why she won't stay on working for me, either,' Harry retorted, then threw up his hands in exasperation. 'I don't know what's going on in Elizabeth's head. I wish I did. I do know that once she makes up her mind, she follows through, so we both have to accept her decision whether we like it or not.'

Michael huffed in frustration. 'Okay,' he conceded. 'It's not your fault.'

'Definitely not,' Harry vehemently insisted.

'Dammit! Why did Lucy have to be her sister?'

'You be careful how you treat her, Mickey. I don't

want your affair with her messing up what I might have
with Elizabeth.'

Michael shook his head over complexities he hadn't
considered. 'We've never been mixed up like this before, Harry.'

'I'll tell you now. I'm not letting Elizabeth go if I
can help it.'

He was deadly serious.

'I'm not about to let Lucy go, either.' Not in the fore-
seeable future. There was absolutely no point to ending it within a month, since Elizabeth wasn't coming
back to work for him. He could let it go on for as long
as it pleased him.

Harry nodded. 'So…are *we* sorted, Mickey?'

'Yes, sorted.'

Which didn't mean he liked the situation, but at least
he agreed Harry wasn't to blame for it. Elizabeth had
pulled the trigger on the professional side, quite possibly swayed by the personal elements of two brothers
and two sisters becoming emotionally entangled. Lucy
had called her *'the sensible one.'*

Michael castigated himself for not seeing this coming, yet he hadn't known the nature of the relationship
between the two sisters when he'd been bowled over by
Lucy last Monday. He'd begun to see it more clearly in
his conversation with Sarah yesterday, but he still hadn't
anticipated this breakaway by Elizabeth.

It seemed an extreme action.

And he resented the assumption that he might treat
Lucy badly.

He had never treated a woman badly.

Yet both Sarah and now Harry were warning him to

be careful with how he treated Lucy. That didn't make a lot of sense, either. She hadn't come across to him as a fragile personality, more like a free spirit, flitting around, trying anything that appealed to her. If their relationship took a wrong turn, surely she would flit somewhere else, not fall in a heap and need massive support from her sister.

Regardless of what he thought or felt, Elizabeth's decision had been made and there was no point in sweating it. He didn't regret picking up with Lucy even if it had lost him his PA. She could become very important to his life—a joy not to be missed or set aside. And he still had three weeks of having her to himself before her sister returned to Cairns—time for the relationship to consolidate, if it was going to—without any outside influence interfering with it.

Michael didn't believe being 'head over heels in love' meant a relationship was on unbreakable ground. It was probably a fair description of how he felt about Lucy right now—infatuated to the point of obsession. But this could be a fairy floss stage, melting into nothing in the end.

He wanted to share a deep, abiding love with a woman.

As his father had with his mother.

He needed more time with Lucy to know if she was *the one* he'd been waiting for.

If she wasn't, he would let her down as lightly as he could.

She might see him as a frog, but he sure as hell wasn't a gross cane toad!

CHAPTER TWELVE

LUCY COULDN'T HELP fretting over the impact of Ellie's decision. The goodbyes after lunch had a strained edge to them, and Harry had called up Jack to drive her and Michael to the jetty in the golf buggy, not choosing to do it himself. She sensed he couldn't see the back of them fast enough, and Lucy was sure he'd be very quickly demanding more explanation from Ellie. He was no longer wearing the expression of a winner.

Michael was harder to read. He chatted to Jack on the way to the jetty in a normal manner, and he held her hand, which was comforting. Jack helped him cast off, and it wasn't until they had left the island behind that Lucy plucked up courage enough to ask, 'Do you feel Ellie has let you down, Michael?'

He made a rueful grimace. 'I can't say I understand her reason for resigning, but every person has the right to choose what to do with their life. I won't argue with that but…she'll be a hard act to follow. It's going to be difficult finding someone to fill her shoes.'

Lucy tried to explain how Ellie might feel. 'I think it has to do with her turning thirty. And the apartment is paid for now, so she doesn't have to feel responsible about keeping a roof over our heads. If you've got that security you can afford to cut free a bit. I guess that's where she's at, Michael.'

He shot her a quizzical look. 'I wondered if it had anything to do with us being connected.'

Lucy shook her head. 'Ellie says not.'

'You asked her?'

'Yes. It just seemed too coincidental somehow. Although I had cleared it with her yesterday morning— like, whatever happens between you and me shouldn't affect what she and Harry could have together. The same should have applied to her job. I told her I'd just pick myself up and move on if it came to us parting.'

His mouth twitched with some private amusement. 'You would, would you?'

'Not easily,' she said archly, pleased that he wasn't grumpy. 'But I would. It's not good to hang on to things that have to be put behind you.'

He laughed, took one hand off the steering wheel of the motor launch and reached out to draw her into a hug. 'That's my Lucy!' he said warmly, and dropped a kiss on her forehead. 'I love the way you look at things.'

Love... Her heart drummed with happiness.

On the work front he was definitely put out by Ellie's resignation, but there was no overflow of negative feeling onto what they had together. He was still a prince to Lucy. She laid her head contentedly on his shoulder and sighed away all her inner angst.

'Thank you for a wonderful weekend, Michael.'

He planted another kiss on her forehead and gave her a tighter hug. '*You* made it wonderful.'

Pure bliss! Michael had passed this test with flying

colours. The only nasty little niggle remaining in her mind was the possible fallout between Ellie and Harry. Lucy *wanted* him to be her sister's prince.

Later that evening, after Michael had left her apartment, she headed straight into Ellie's room to email her. The great thing about modern technology was the common practice of using shorthand texting that cut out a lot of letters in words. Lucy could manage this simplified communication fairly well, though Ellie could get the gist of any garbled stuff she typed, so it wasn't a problem, anyway.

She kept it short.

M & I R OK. R U & H OK?

As soon as she woke up the next morning she rushed to the computer hoping for an answer. A new message popped into the inbox and yes, it was from Ellie. It opened with a smile sign, which instantly put a smile on Lucy's face, then the confirmation: H & I OK.

Still two princes, Lucy thought happily, and the week passed brilliantly without anything happening to put even a slight crack in that sweet belief. It gave her more confidence about going to the ball with Michael. She was sure he would smooth over any shortcomings she might have in the company of his friends.

On Saturday he took her out to lunch, saying they probably wouldn't be fed until quite late tonight so they might as well enjoy a good meal early in the afternoon and have plenty of energy for dancing. He drove them to the Thala Beach Lodge, which was located between

Cairns and Port Douglas and perched on top of a steep hill with magnificent views of the coast and sea.

The restaurant was open-air, with high wooden ceilings and polished floorboards, and their table for two overlooked the rainforest that covered the hillside down to the beach. Lucy once again covered up her dyslexia, remarking to the waitress that everything on the menu looked marvellous, and asking what were the most popular choices. That made it easy to pounce on the coconut prawns, followed by a chocolate fudge brownie with pistachio nuts, roasted banana and butterscotch sauce. This time it was Michael who chose to have 'the same', which gave Lucy a pleasant sense of complacency about her disability.

Maybe he would never notice it, or by the time he did, hopefully he wouldn't care about it, because there was so much that was good between them.

Like enjoying this delicious lunch together.

Like making love back in her apartment until she had to chase Michael off so she could do all she had to do to look her absolute best for the ball.

Lucy didn't own a ball gown. She had thought of borrowing one of the costumes from the dance studio where she'd worked, but decided the competition creations might look out of place in a crowd that was bound to be sophisticated. In the end, her tangerine bridesmaid dress seemed the best choice. It was a simple, long, figure-hugging shift with a knee-high split at the back for ease of movement. The square neckline was low enough to show the upper swell of her breasts—definitely an evening gown look—and the straps over the shoulders were linked by three gold rings.

With the honey-tan tone of her skin, blond hair and brown eyes, the tangerine colour looked great on her, and the garment was spectacular enough in itself not to need much dressing up—just gold hoop earrings, her slimline gold watch, the gold bangle Ellie had given her on her twenty-first birthday, the gold strappy sandals that were perfect dancing shoes, and a small gold handbag for essential make-up repair items.

She washed and blow-dried her hair, twirling it up into a topknot, and using a curling wand on the loose tendrils that dangled down from it. She kept her make-up fairly subtle, carefully highlighting her eyes and cheekbones, wanting to look right for the company she was to be in tonight, but she did gloss her tangerine lipstick. The dress demanded it and she wanted to look right for herself, too.

Certainly Michael had no problem with her appearance. When he arrived to pick her up he took one look at her and shook his head in awe, murmuring, 'You take my breath away.' Then he gave her a sparkling grin, adding, 'Not for the first time!'

She laughed. 'You do the same to me.'

He was always stunningly handsome, but dressed in a formal dinner suit he was truly breathtaking. Excited simply to be with him, Lucy stopped worrying about other people. She was going to dance all night with this beautiful, fantastic man and have a wonderful time.

However, her exhilaration was inevitably overtaken by nervous tension as they entered the casino ballroom, the need for Michael's friends to find her acceptable rising with every step she took. She tried to reassure herself with the fact that Sarah and Jack Pickard had liked her, but they had been an older couple, probably not as inclined to be as critical as a peer group.

The table Michael led her to was half occupied. They obviously weren't the first of the party to arrive, nor the last. The men stood as Michael started the introductions, and Lucy did her best to fit the names she had memorised to the faces. These were the three married couples he'd told her about, and they eyed her with interest—a new woman on the scene.

'Where did you meet this gorgeous lady, Mickey?' one of the men asked.

'She burst in on me at work and I instantly decided...' his eyes twinkled at Lucy '...I needed her in my life.'

Her heart swelled with happiness at this public declaration.

'Ah! A business connection then,' his friend concluded.

'You could say that. Though my connection to Lucy now extends way beyond business.' He gave her a hug. 'I'm here to dance her off her feet tonight.'

They all laughed. One of the women archly commented, 'He is a very good dancer, Lucy. If you can't keep up with him, hand him over to me.'

'No chance!' Michael told her. 'Lucy has done the dance studio thing. I'm out to prove I can match her.'

'Well, you look like a good match,' another woman remarked, smiling at both of them.

Lucy no longer felt tense and nervous. They were all looking at her in a friendly manner, willing to accept her into their company. Michael had set them on that path with his admiring comments, and they were happy to go along with him. Like a true prince, he'd made the situation easy for her, and she had no trouble carrying on a conversation with these people, using the information he'd given about them to focus on their lives and interests.

Once the band started up, he swept her off to the dance floor. He had great rhythm and was so sexy, Lucy could barely contain the excitement he stirred in her. Dance followed dance. He challenged her with intricate moves and she challenged him right back. Other couples made more room for them on the floor, standing back to watch and applaud their display of expertise. It was wildly exhilarating and they were both breathless when the set ended and they made their way back to the table.

The rest of their party had arrived. More introductions were made. Lucy was on too much of a high to feel nervous about them. Besides, they were all grinning at them, with one commenting, 'You two are hot, hot, hot! That was a sizzling performance on the dance floor.'

Michael laughed. 'I've never had a partner like Lucy.'

'And he's so good I'm only just still on my feet,' she said, sliding her arm around his waist and leaning into him as though close to collapse.

He hugged her shoulders and glanced inquiringly at the men. 'Who's pouring the champagne? My lady needs a refreshing drink.'

Champagne, dancing, fun company, the burgeoning hope that Michael might see her as a partner in every sense… Lucy realised the concern about being a Cinderella at this ball was completely wiped out. She felt like a princess. Not even a clash with Michael's ex in the powder room could dim the stars in her eyes.

The unexpected confrontation with the beautiful brunette was not pleasant. Lucy was refreshing her lipstick at the vanity mirror when the woman beside her turned to face her with a spiteful glare.

'Just who are you?' she demanded.

Startled, Lucy retorted, 'Who are *you?*'

'Fiona Redman.'

The name meant nothing to Lucy. 'So?'

'Michael Finn was mine until a month ago,' she spat out. 'I want to know if you're the reason he dropped me.'

'No. I've only known him for two weeks.'

She gnashed her teeth over that information, her dark eyes glowering meanly at Lucy. 'Well, don't expect to keep him. He's notoriously fickle in his relationships. Business always comes first with him.'

Lucy made no reply. She was recalling Michael's description of this woman as too self-centred.

'He might be as handsome as sin and great in bed, but he'll just use you and toss you away like all the rest,' the woman jeered.

'Thank you for warning me,' Lucy said politely, and made a quick escape, smiling over her mother's old saying, 'the soft word turneth away wrath.' It had always worked for her, putting people off their rants. It was obvious that Fiona Redman was as jealous as sin, having lost 'her catch', and Lucy was not about to let her spoil this brilliant night with Michael.

He hadn't let Jason Lester spoil anything between them.

What they had together was special. It had nothing to do with anyone else. Michael's past relationships simply hadn't proved *right,* just as hers hadn't. As far as Lucy was concerned, a small future with each other remained shining brightly at this point in time.

Michael had taken the opportunity to visit the men's room while Lucy was in the ladies', not wanting to lose any time together. He was washing his hands when another guy claimed his attention, sliding a highly provocative comment at him.

'I see you've snagged the best piece of arse in Cairns.'

Michael frowned at him. 'I beg your pardon.'

'Luscious Lucy.' This was accompanied by a leer. 'Great for sex. Pity she's such an airhead. I enjoyed her for a while. I'm sure you will, too. But trying to put some order into her mess of a mind wore me out.'

The control freak, Michael thought.

The guy flicked water off his hands and made one last rotten comment. 'She should keep her mouth for what it's good at.'

He walked out, leaving Michael untroubled by the 'airhead' tag, but disturbed at having Lucy described as 'the best piece of arse in Cairns.' It made him recall Jason Lester's remark that she'd slept with half the men in the city. Michael didn't believe this was true, certain that Lucy had more discrimination than that, yet it once more raised the question of how many men she had pleasured in the past, and how she had learnt to give so much pleasure.

He told himself it didn't matter.

He revelled in her uninhibited sensuality, her utterly spontaneous response to the sexual chemistry between them. He was glad she was like that, and however it had come about should not concern him. Apart from which, the disparaging comments had come from men Lucy had rejected—men who were missing out on what they wanted from her.

Michael returned to their table, determined to banish the niggles about her past. If she was hiding things she didn't want him to know…so what? He liked what he had with her in the present, and wasn't about to mess with it.

She was already seated, her lovely face alight with interest in the conversation amongst his friends. He took the empty chair across the table from her for the sheer pleasure of watching her smiles, the dimples flashing in her cheeks, the golden twinkles in her sherry-brown eyes, the slight heave of her perfect breasts when she laughed.

Luscious Lucy…

The phrase slid into his mind and stuck there.

They were served a seafood banquet. He watched the sensual way she forked oysters into her mouth, the relish with which she ate chunks of lobster, the licking of her lips to capture any escaping dipping sauce with the prawns, the sheer love of good food that shone through her enjoyment of the sumptuous supper.

Luscious Lucy…

There couldn't be a man alive who wouldn't think of her in those terms. Everything about her was sexy. Michael was strongly aroused simply watching her. It was difficult to contain the desire she stirred in him, the need stealing his appetite, making him impatient for the stack of gourmet food to be eaten and cleared away.

Finally the band started up again. They began with a slow number—a jazz waltz. *Perfect,* Michael thought, gesturing in invitation to Lucy as he rose from his chair. While he skirted the table, she rose from hers, as eager as he was for physical connection. He took her hand. She squeezed his. A few strides and he was swinging her into his embrace, holding her close, legs brushing against each other in the sensual intimacy of the dance.

He was acutely conscious of his erection furrowing her stomach, her breasts pressing into his chest, the warmth of her breath feathering the skin of his neck. He wanted her so badly it was almost a sickness inside him. He wanted her to himself, completely to himself.

The control mechanism in his mind snapped.

The question that should have stayed unasked came out of his mouth in a harsh rasp.

'How many men have you slept with, Lucy?'

She stopped dancing with him.

Her hands slid down to his chest, pushing to create distance between them. She looked up, stared at his face, her eyes blank of all expression, as though she was staring through him at something else.

And Michael knew instantly what it was.

The frog inside him.

He could almost feel himself turning green, and though he wanted to push back that fatal tide of colour, it was impossible to erase the words he had spoken. They hung between them, waiting to be answered— words that might well cost him a woman he wanted to keep in his life.

He wasn't ready to lose Lucy.

He might never be ready to lose her.

She'd become an addiction he didn't want to end.

CHAPTER THIRTEEN

LUCY FELT SICK.

She couldn't understand why Michael had asked that question now, on this night of nights, when everything had seemed so good between them. She had expected it—dreaded it—a week ago when Jason Lester had made that crack about her having slept with half the men in Cairns, which she had made worse with her 'town slut' remark.

Her stomach roiled with nausea.

Had she done something *sluttish* tonight? Lucy frantically searched her mind for some word or action of hers that might have triggered bad thoughts along those lines.

Nothing.

She'd simply been herself.

And if Michael couldn't accept her for the person she was...

'It doesn't matter!' he fiercely muttered. 'Forget I asked, Lucy. It was a stupid question.'

It jerked her into refocusing, meeting his eyes, searching them for truth. 'It does matter to me, Michael,' she quietly stated, hating the fact that he might think her indiscriminately promiscuous.

He grimaced in self-disgust. 'I ran into your latest ex—the control freak—in the men's room. He made some remarks about you. I shouldn't have let what he said bother me, but coming on top of Lester's...' Michael shook his head as though trying to rid his mind of images he didn't want there.

'People who want to cast nasty aspersions on others usually make sex the centre of them. Especially men, I've found. But women, too,' Lucy said, instinctively mounting a counter-attack out of a desperate need to defend herself. 'I was confronted by *your* ex—Fiona Redman—in the ladies' room. Her words were you were great in bed, but you used women up and tossed them away.' Lucy summoned up a wry little smile. 'I didn't believe you were so callous.'

'I'm sorry,' he declared. 'It's just that you're...' He paused, struggling to explain, probably hating that he'd put himself in the position of having to explain.

'What, Michael? Does it bother you that I feel free to enjoy sex as much as you do?'

'No!' He sliced the air with his hand—a sharp, negative gesture. His eyes blazed with intensity of feeling. 'I love how you are with me, Lucy.'

Not enough, she thought. *Not enough.*

Her stomach started cramping.

She clutched it, trying to stop the rolling of pain. Something was wrong. This wasn't just emotional stress. It was too physical. Had she eaten something that was violently disagreeing with her?

Defiantly determined to finish what Michael had started, she lifted her chin and faced him with her truth. 'To answer your question—'

'Don't!' he commanded tersely.

She went on, disregarding his denial of any need for it. 'I've probably slept with as many men as you have women. I've seen no reason not to have the pleasure of sex when it promised to be pleasurable. I've found each experience quite different, because the men were different. And when it came it you, Michael, it was very special.' Tears spurted into her eyes. 'So special...'

Her throat choked up. Her stomach heaved. Bile shot into her mouth. She turned blindly, desperate to get to the ladies' room before she started vomiting.

Strong hands gripped her shoulders, halting any attempt at flight. 'Lucy...' It was a gruff plea.

'I'm sick! I'm going to be sick!' she cried, clapping her hand over her mouth as she doubled over, pain shafting her lower body.

No more talk. Nothing but action, Michael moving her, supporting her, collecting one of his friends along the way to look after her in the ladies' room. Lucy barely had time to sink down on her knees in a toilet cubicle before the contents of her stomach erupted. The convulsions kept coming, even when there was nothing left to vomit. Then she was hit by diarrhoea and that was just as bad. It felt as though her whole lovely night was going down the toilet, along with the relationship she'd hoped to have with Michael Finn.

Michael waited outside the ladies' room, anxious over Lucy's condition and cursing himself for probably contributing to her sudden bout of illness with his stupid question about other men. Everything she'd said back to him was totally reasonable. *Totally.* He should have known it without asking. He should have realised that a free spirit like Lucy would take what she wanted from life and not feel she had to account for it to anyone else. And neither should she.

He'd acted like a jealous man instead of being grateful for having her light up his life, and any sense of jealousy appalled him. It was not the attribute of a rational man, which he'd always prided himself on being. This overwhelming obsession with Lucy had to stop. It was getting out of hand. He needed to pull back from it, be less intense about the feelings she stirred in him.

Though he might very well have wrecked any choice to do anything about it.

Was he now an irredeemable frog in her eyes?

Certainly, he'd killed the light in them—the light that had told him he was special.

She was special.

And he desperately wanted another chance with her.

If she walked away from him tonight, shut the door on him…

His hands clenched. He had to fight, win her back, convince her he would never again make the mistake of holding her to account for anything she might have done before they'd met. Only what they had together was important. That was what he cared about. The future without her in it looked too empty of any joy to even contemplate such an outcome. He would not accept it.

The door to the ladies' room opened. He'd asked Dave Whitfield's wife, Jane, to do what she could for Lucy, and it was a relief to see her coming out. He needed to know what state Lucy was in, whether there was some positive action he could take. Every fibre of his being was intent on changing the situation as it stood.

Jane made a sympathetic grimace. 'Not good, I'm afraid. She's violently ill. I think it must be food poisoning, though the rest of us seem to be fine. Maybe there was a bad oyster in the seafood banquet, and Lucy lucked out, being the one to eat it.'

'What should I do?' Michael asked, feeling helplessly locked out of doing anything.

'I think you'll either have to take her to hospital emergency or…does she have someone to look after her at home?'

'I'll look after her.'

'She might need some medication, Mickey. I'll go back and stay with her until she's okay to get moving.' Jane frowned. 'Though if this keeps up we might have to call an ambulance. I'll let you know if that's the case.'

'Thanks, Jane.'

'It's such a shame!' She shook her head over the mishap as she turned back to the ladies' room.

Shame was right, Michael thought savagely. Shame on him for causing more upset to Lucy when she had started to feel unwell. He had to make up for it, be all she needed him to be. The minutes dragging by felt like hours as he waited for more news. Other women entered and left the ladies' room, glancing curiously at him as they passed. He didn't care what they thought. Only Lucy mattered. He remained on watch.

Finally the door opened and Jane shuffled out, supporting Lucy, who looked completely debilitated—with no colour in her face at all. Even the bright orange lipstick had been wiped off. Her eyes were bleary, as though they'd been washed by a river of tears. Her shoulders were slumped and it was obvious she was too physically drained to stand up straight.

Michael moved quickly to draw her to his side, taking over Jane's supporting role. There was no resistance to his action. Michael suspected she was grateful to have anyone holding on to her.

'She wants to go home, Mickey,' Jane informed him. 'I think the worst is over, but she's fairly shaky. I'll get her bag and fetch Dave. If you give him your keys and tell him where you've parked, he can drive your car to the front of the casino, ready for you to put Lucy in. Okay?'

He nodded. 'Thanks, Jane.'

There was so much he wanted to say to Lucy. but she was in no condition to listen, and he knew it would be selfish of him to push any issues in these circumstances. She needed kindness and comfort.

Jane quickly organised the easiest possible exit from the casino, accompanying them to the car, which Dave had waiting for them. She opened the passenger door and Michael lifted Lucy into the seat and secured her safety belt.

Lucy mumbled 'Thank you' to everyone. Michael quickly expressed his gratitude for his friends' help, anxious to get her home. She was so limp and listless, he worried over whether to take her to the hospital instead as he settled in the driver's seat and started the engine.

'Are you sure you don't need medical attention, Lucy?' he asked.

'Just want to lie down and sleep,' she answered, sounding exhausted.

It was probably the best option, he thought as he set off for her apartment. There wasn't much comfort in waiting for attention in a queue at the emergency room of a hospital, and maybe the worst was over. She wasn't sick during the trip home. Once there, he took her keys out of her bag and carried her into the apartment—a move she weakly protested wasn't needed, but he did it anyway, wanting to hold her in his arms.

He stood her up beside her bed, unzipped her dress, slid it off her arms so it could drop to her feet, before he sat her down and worked on removing her underclothes and gold sandals. Her skin felt hot and she shivered several times, obviously feverish. He picked out the pins holding up her hair, running his fingers through the falling tresses to ensure they were all gone, before gently lowering her to the pillows, lifting her feet onto the bed and tucking the doona around her.

'Good of you, Michael,' she murmured with a ragged sigh. 'It's okay for you to go now. Thank you.'

She closed her eyes, and the sense of being shut out of her life twisted Michael's gut. If she'd consigned him to the frog species, according to the fairy tale, the only way to change that was for her to kiss him, willingly and caringly. Somehow he had to win his way back into her heart, persuade her to overlook his crass question as totally irrelevant to their relationship. Which it truly was.

'I'm not leaving you,' he muttered with fierce determination, sitting on the bed beside her and gently stroking her hair away from her hot forehead. 'You're not okay, Lucy. You're running a fever. Do you have any medication here that might lower your temperature?'

She sighed again, whether in exasperation at his

persistence or with her illness, he couldn't tell. Her eyelashes lifted slightly as she answered, 'Bathroom cupboard.'

Her voice was flat. The slitted look she gave him revealed nothing of what she was feeling towards him. 'I'll find it,' he said, and went to the bathroom.

There was a packet of pain tablets that were supposed to lower fever. He took them and went to the kitchen to fill a glass with water before returning to Lucy. He lifted her up from the pillows, fed her the tablets and held the glass to her lips. She gulped down some water. Michael was thinking she was probably dehydrated when she suddenly hurled off the doona, erupted from the bed and staggered towards the bathroom.

Apparently her stomach couldn't tolerate anything in it. Michael had to stand by helplessly as she was convulsively sick again. 'I think I'd better take you to hospital, Lucy,' he said worriedly.

'No…no…' She shook her head vehemently. 'Just help me back to bed. I'll sleep it off.'

Did she want to sleep him off, too?

What could he say?

What could he do?

He tried to make her comfortable again. He dampened a face-cloth and laid it across her forehead, then remembered the cup of ice Harry had been given to suck when he was in hospital with a broken nose. Lucy was definitely dehydrated. He found a tray of ice cubes in the freezer, emptied most of it into a large tumbler and set it on her bedside table. Her eyes were closed again. Not wanting to leave her without any ready access for help, he took her mobile telephone out of her gold hand-bag and laid it on the bedside table, too.

'Listen to me, Lucy,' he said urgently. 'I'm going to the all-night chemist to ask the pharmacist for advice. Hopefully, he'll have something to settle your stomach. I'll be back soon. Try to suck some of the ice I've left here for you. I've put your phone within easy reach, as well, so you can call me if you need to. Okay?'

'Okay.'

It was barely a whisper of sound. Michael thought she was beyond caring. He hurried out to his car and drove towards the centre of town, where he knew the all-night chemist shop was situated. He was still in two minds about overriding her decision and taking her to hospital. The most important thing right now was to get her well again. Then he could work at making her understand how special she was to him.

He didn't see the car coming at him from the street to his right. The traffic lights at the intersection were green his way. He was focused on where he was going and what he had to do. He felt the impact, then nothing else. All consciousness ceased.

CHAPTER FOURTEEN

THERE WAS A persistent tune penetrating the fog in Lucy's sleep-laden head. On and on it went, until she was conscious enough to realise it was the call-tune of her mobile telephone. Still groggy, she flung an arm out to the bedside table, fumbled around until her hand found the source of irritation. She wanted to shut it off, but some vague memory of Michael leaving the phone beside her to call him made her lift it to her ear.

'Yes...what?' The words emerged in a slurred fashion. Her mouth was dreadfully dry. Her tongue felt furred. It was a huge effort to speak at all.

'Wake up, Lucy!' someone ordered sharply. 'There's been an accident.'

A woman's voice. It sounded like her sister. And saying something about an accident. On the island?

Lucy hauled herself into a sitting position and tried to concentrate. Having pried her eyes open, she could see there was some very early-morning light coming from her window, but it was still an ungodly hour to call anyone.

'What?' she asked again. 'Is that you, Ellie?'

'Yes. Michael was injured in a car accident early this morning. He was badly hurt.'

'Michael…oh, no… No…' Shock cleared her mind in no time flat. The memory of him bringing her home, looking after her, going out to get something for her stomach shot straight into it. 'Oh, God!' she wailed. 'It's my fault!'

'How is it your fault?' Ellie asked worriedly.

'I ate something at dinner last night that upset me. He brought me home. I was vomiting and had dreadful diarrhoea. He left me to find an all-night pharmacy to get me some medicine. I was so drained I must have drifted off to sleep. He should have come back, but he's not here and… Oh, God! He went out for me, Ellie!'

'Stop that, Lucy! You didn't cause the accident, and getting hysterical won't help Michael,' she said vehemently, cutting off the futile guilt trip. 'I take it everything was still good between you last night?'

'Yes…yes… He was so caring when I was sick. Oh, Ellie! I'll die if I lose him.'

She forgot she had probably already lost him. All she could think of was how special he was, how much she loved him.

'Then you'd better do whatever you can to make him want to live,' Ellie sharply advised. 'Are you still sick? Can you get to the hospital? He's in an intensive care unit.'

'I'll get there.' Gritty determination quelled every vestige of hysterical panic.

'Harry was with me on the island,' Ellie went on. 'He's on his way. Be kind to him, Lucy. Remember he and Michael lost their parents in an accident. I have to stay here. Harry's counting on me to take care of business, but I think he'll need someone there, too.'

'I understand. You love him but you can't be with him.'

At least that was good—Ellie and Harry teaming up together. Lucy couldn't let herself dwell on where she and Michael were in their relationship when he was fighting for his life in an intensive care unit.

'I need to know what's happening, Lucy,' Ellie said in a softer tone. 'Please…will you keep me informed?'

'Sure!' Clearly, the situation deeply concerned her sister, too, with Michael being Harry's brother, as well as a man she had worked closely with for two years. 'I'll call you with news as soon as I have it. Moving now. Over and out. Okay?'

'Okay.'

Moving was not easy. Lucy was still weak and shaky. Her head whirled as she forced her legs to take her to the bathroom. Nothing in her stomach, she thought, but was too scared of being sick again to eat or drink anything. Somehow she had to make it to the hospital and not look like the total wreck she saw in the vanity mirror.

Slowly, carefully, she cleaned herself up, brushed her hair and applied some make-up to put colour in her face. Bright clothes, she decided, wanting to make Michael smile…if he was up to smiling at all. She refused to let herself think he might die, though it was impossible to banish the anxiety spearing pain through her heart.

It took a while to put clothes on, since she needed to sit down more than once until her rockiness subsided. She selected the yellow wraparound dress to remind him of the great sex they'd shared, and the pretty shell necklace that might recall their wonderful time together on Finn Island. He would surely want to live to have those pleasures again.

Being in no condition to drive safely, she called for a taxi to pick her up and take her to the hospital. On the trip there she kept wondering where the accident had happened, and how it could have been so serious when traffic in the city had to move at a relatively slow pace. Had Michael been speeding, wanting to get back to her quickly? Had she unwittingly been the cause of it?

Her mind was awash with tormenting questions when she finally arrived at the intensive care unit. Before she could properly inquire about Michael at the nurses' station, Harry suddenly appeared at her side and swept her off to the waiting room, his grim expression filling her with fear. He sat her down and stood over her as he gave her the information she most needed to know.

'It's not too bad, Lucy. His injuries aren't life-threatening. He was hit on the driver's side, right arm and hip fractured, broken ribs, lacerations to the face, a lot of bruising, concussion. The doctors were worried that a broken rib had punctured his liver, but that's been cleared, and bones will mend.' Harry's sigh transmitted a mountain of relief. 'He's going to be incapacitated for quite a while, but there should be no lasting damage.'

'Thank God!' Her own relief was mountainous, as well. 'How did it happen, Harry?' She was still anxious to know that.

'Drunken teenagers in a stolen car ran a red light and slammed into him as he was driving across an intersection. They're all here, too. Needless to say, I don't have much sympathy for them.'

Another huge roll of relief. The accident wasn't Michael's fault. Nor hers. It was simply a case of being in the wrong place at the wrong time, although he wouldn't have been there but for her. Still, the food poisoning was an accident, too, and there was no point in fretting over it. Moving on was the only way to go.

'Can I go and see Michael now?'

Harry grimaced. 'I don't think that's a good idea.'

'Why not?'

'Well, to put it bluntly, he's barely recognisable. It will come as a shock to you. They've stitched the cuts on his face, but it's very bruised and swollen. He's also sedated to keep the pain at bay, and it's best if he stays that way. If you start screaming or carrying on—'

She cut him off very sharply. 'Harry Finn, I nursed my mother while she slowly died from cancer. Nothing is worse than seeing someone you love wasting away. I am no wimp when it comes to facing people who are suffering, and I am not stupid. I care a lot about Michael and no way would I do anything to wake him up to pain. I just want to be with him.'

Surprise at her vehemence gave way to a look of respect for her. He nodded. 'Then I'll take you to him.'

'Good!'

She pushed herself up from the chair and steadied herself for the walk to Michael's bedside. Harry took her arm, which helped her stay reasonably steady. 'Have you called Ellie to let her know Michael will come through this?' she asked, as he led her back to the intensive care unit.

'Not yet. I've just finished talking to the doctors. Since there's no critical danger, they won't operate on

Mickey until tomorrow morning. I've insisted on the top surgeon.'

'I'm glad about that, but do call my sister, Harry. She's anxiously waiting for news.'

'As soon as you're settled with Mickey,' he promised.

It was better if Ellie heard everything from Harry, Lucy thought. She would call her sister tonight, hopefully after Michael had woken up and she had more personal news.

Harry certainly hadn't exaggerated Michael's facial injuries. Seeing him did come as a shock, but she swiftly told herself all this was a temporary phase. He would heal. Harry pulled up a chair for her to sit beside the bed, and she sank gratefully onto it, reaching out to take Michael's left hand in hers, mindful that his right arm had been broken. His flesh was warm. No matter how ghastly he looked, he was alive, and she fiercely willed him to want her in his future.

Though she wasn't sure how much of a future he would want with her. His questioning last night about how many men she had slept with had not left her with a good feeling. It seemed judgemental in a nasty way. He'd told her to forget it, that it didn't matter, but he had brought it up so it obviously meant something to him. Had her answer satisfied him?

She'd become too ill to assess his reaction to it. Whatever he'd thought, he'd been good to her, sticking around, bringing her home, doing his best to look after her. Still a prince, in that sense. She could only hope there wasn't a frog lurking inside him.

Her head ached. Harry had left the room, probably

to make the call to Ellie. Lucy felt too tired to think anymore. Besides, it seemed pointless. There would be no answers until Michael woke up. She rested her head on the bed beside the hand she was holding. The effort to get here had drained her of what little energy she had after being so sick. She slid into sleep without realising it was happening.

A hand gripping hers hard jerked her awake. Michael's swollen black eyes were opened into thin slits. Having drawn her attention, he croaked out, 'Where am I?'

'In hospital, Mickey,' Harry answered, rising from a chair on the other side of the bed to put himself in his brother's line of sight. 'Don't move,' he commanded. 'You have broken bones.'

'How? Why? I can't open my eyes much.'

'You were in a car accident and your face copped a beating. So did your body,' Harry told him bluntly.

'How bad?'

'You'll mend, but it will take some time.'

'It hurts to breathe.'

'Broken ribs.'

'Car accident... I can't remember.'

'Concussion. The doctors warned me you might not regain any memory of last night.'

Lucy shot an inquiring glance at Harry. He hadn't told her that. How much memory might be blotted out? And would it stay blotted out?

He nodded to her. 'Lucy's here. I'll go and fetch the doctor on duty. I was told to do that as soon as you were conscious. He'll answer any questions you have, Mickey.'

Michael squeezed her hand as he shifted his limited vision to her. 'Lucy,' he said, as though he loved her name.

She squeezed back, smiling at him. 'You're going to be okay,' she assured him.

'I remember we had lunch at the Thala Beach Lodge. What happened last night?'

'We went to a ball at the casino. We danced for hours until they served a seafood banquet. Something I ate gave me food poisoning. You took me home, then went out to an all-night chemist to get me some medication. Harry told me a stolen car slammed into you at an intersection—a drunken driver running a red light.'

He shook his head slightly and winced. 'I don't remember any of that.'

'Don't worry about it.'

'Food poisoning…last night… You must feel wretched, Lucy.'

Her heart turned over. Here he was, caring about her when he was all broken up and obviously hurting.

'I'll live,' she said dismissively. 'I had to see you, be with you, Michael. Ellie called me with the news and I was frightened you might not make it through.' She smiled to lighten up the situation. 'I was going to hang on to you like grim death until you did.'

'That's my girl,' he said with a ghost of a smile.

It was so blissful to hear him say that, as though nothing had changed between them.

Harry returned with the doctor and Lucy moved out of the way of any medical checking that had to be done, standing at the end of the bed and holding the foot railing for support. She did feel wretched. A glance at her

The only bright spot in his current life was Lucy.

He was intensely grateful she had decided to overlook his frog blunder at the ball, calling into question her sexual experience. He still didn't remember the car accident, but memories of everything preceding it had come swimming back to him after the hip operation.

He'd actually been afraid she wouldn't visit him again, since he wasn't about to die, but she had turned up on Monday evening and every evening since, chatting to him in her wonderfully bubbly fashion, massaging his feet, giving him her beautiful smile, not at all concerned that he looked like Frankenstein's monster.

Michael had been moved to a private room with his own television to make time pass less tediously. He had no complaints about the care given to him from the medical staff. The physiotherapist was particularly good. His friends dropped in to see him, bringing him gifts to keep him in reasonably good cheer. Harry kept him informed of business issues and was always good company. But it was Lucy who brought sunshine into his room. She made him feel lucky to be alive and very lucky to have her in his life.

Today he was glad it was Saturday, not a workday for her, and she'd promised to visit him this morning. While he waited for her he struggled with the newspaper he'd asked to be delivered to him. It was the *Sydney Morning Herald* and its pages were large. Having the use of only one arm, handling them was awkward, and most of them slid off the bed onto the floor as he tried o separate out the financial section, which he liked to ad each week.

He finally managed it, and having found an article

watch told her she'd actually slept with her head on Michael's bed for over three hours, which should have helped, yet her legs were still weak and shaky.

The doctor went through a schedule of procedures, explaining what would be done and when. He answered questions, then administered an injection of morphine before he left.

Michael turned his attention to her. 'You must go home and rest, Lucy. You need recovery time from food poisoning, and I'll probably be out of it for most of today and tomorrow.' He shifted his gaze to his brother. 'Make her go, Harry.'

'I will,' he promised.

She didn't want to, but saw the sense in it. 'I'll go,' she said, moving around to his side to take his hand again, pressing it with fervent caring. 'I'll come back tomorrow evening. I hope the operation goes well, Michael.'

'Don't worry about it. Hip operations are run-of-the-mill stuff these days.'

She leaned over and kissed his lips very softly. 'I'll be thinking of you every minute,' she murmured.

Harry accompanied her out of the hospital and put her in a taxi. 'Take care of yourself, Lucy,' he said kindly. 'I think my brother will need you in the difficult days to come.'

It was nice that he thought she was an important part of Michael's life. Maybe she still could be if Michael never remembered questioning her about past sexual partners. Initially he had dismissed the Jason Lester encounter. It was the run-in with her most recent ex last night that had reignited the issue in his mind. If that was now wiped out… Lucy couldn't help hoping everything would be right between them.

She desperately wanted to hold on to her prince.

She couldn't bear it if he turned into a frog.

CHAPTER FIFTEEN

FOR MICHAEL IT was a hell of a week. The broken arm was a nuisance because he couldn't use it. The broken ribs gave him pain with every movement, and he had to move. The nurses got him out of bed every day after the hip operation, walking up and down a corridor to ensure his muscles kept working around the piece of titanium that had been inserted.

On top of that was his frustration at having to leave his business to Harry, who was making a good fist of handling the franchises under his instructions, but didn't have the sense of creativity needed to take any new initiatives. Which wasn't really a problem. That could wait for Michael's return. He simply wasn't use to not controlling everything himself. It would ha been easier for Harry if Elizabeth had been on han the perfect PA—but she was stepping in for him o island while he was tied up here.

The accident couldn't have come at a wors incapacitating Michael when he had no one i fice he trusted to take over in any capacity wh Andrew Cook was next to useless, needing s tell him everything, and there hadn't been a competent replacement for Elizabeth.

that interested him, he was frustrated again by his vision blurring over the little print. Probably an after-effect of the concussion, he reasoned. The swelling had gone down and his eyes were back to normal, but this was obviously yet another thing he would have to wait out.

He was darkly brooding over the frustrating aspects of his situation when Lucy walked in, all bright and beautiful, instantly lifting his spirits. She'd put up her hair in a kind of tousled topknot, and her eyes were sparkling, her dimples flashing, her smile totally enchanting. She was wearing purple jeans teamed with a purple-lime-and-white top in a wildly floral print, long dangly purple-and-lime earrings and a set of matching bangles.

He smiled. 'You look fantastic, Lucy!'

She laughed. 'I like dressing up. It's fun.'

Fun like a carnival full of happy surprises, he thought.

She'd brought him a surprise, too, holding out to him a perfect yellow rose in a long-stemmed glass vase.

'Look! Isn't it beautiful, Michael? I was out at the cemetery yesterday and the old man who planted a Pal Joey rose on his wife's grave was there. He cut this off for me, but it wasn't quite in full bloom so I waited until today to bring it to you.' She placed the vase on his bedside table. 'Just the glorious scent of it will take away the hospital antiseptic smell and make you feel better.'

'I'm sure it will. Thank you, Lucy.'

'My pleasure.'

She leaned over and kissed him. Desire for her had already kicked in and he wished he could crush her to him, but his ribs were still a problem, so he had to suffer her moving away to pull up a chair.

'Wow! You've made a mess of this newspaper,' she said, bending over to shuffle the dropped pages into a manageable bundle.

It reminded him of the article he'd wanted to read, which was still on his bed, and he needed a distraction from the rush of hot blood Lucy stirred with her sexy derriere bobbing around. 'Just leave them in a pile and sit down, Lucy. There's something I want you to read to me. The little print has me defeated at the moment. My vision keeps blurring. It's an article in this financial section.' He picked it up and held it out to her.

She took it somewhat gingerly and sat down, frowning at the opened page. 'The financial section,' she repeated slowly, sounding troubled. She looked up with a quick, appealing smile. 'Wouldn't it be better if Harry read it to you? Then you could discuss whatever's in it together. I'm simply not into that scene, Michael.'

'Harry has gone over to the island with the guy who's to take over the job of manager as soon as Elizabeth can train him into the job. I don't expect him back until tomorrow. Besides, I don't want to discuss it,' he argued. 'I simply want to know what it says. It's been annoying me, not being able to read it. It will only take five minutes, Lucy. Please?'

The smile was gone. She gave him an anguished look. 'I'd really rather not.'

'Why not?'

Surely it was only a small favour to ask. Why put it off? Why was it a problem to her? She'd lowered her lashes to hide the strange anguish he'd seen, and her body was tensing up as though readying itself to spring from the chair. All this was incomprehensible to him.

'Lucy?' he pressed, needing to have her odd reaction cleared up.

She slowly set the section of newspaper he'd given her on the bed, drawing her hands back to pick at each other nervously in her lap. She drew in a deep breath, then met his gaze squarely as though facing a feared inquisitor.

'I can't, Michael,' she said flatly.

Still it made no sense to him. 'What do you mean... you *can't?*'

Her chin lifted slightly. 'I was born with dyslexia. I've always had difficulty with reading and writing.'

Dyslexia...

He didn't know much about it, only that letters in words got jumbled up to people who had that disability.

Lucy gave a wry little shrug. 'I can usually wing my way through most situations.' Her eyes were bleak with vulnerability as she added, 'But I've been sacked from jobs because of it and dumped from relationships because of it. I know I'm no match for you, Michael. I just wanted to have you love me for a little while.' Tears glittered. 'And you have, quite beautifully.'

It sounded perilously close to a goodbye speech to Michael. 'Now hold on a moment!' He cut in fast and hard. 'This isn't the end for us. I won't have it, Lucy. You're my girl, regardless. What I want is for you to tell me about your dyslexia. Share it with me. You don't have to hide it from me.'

She bit her lips. Her head drooped. Her eyelashes worked overtime, trying to blink away the tears. Her distress was heart-wrenching. She was such a beautiful person, and clearly this disability had been a blight on her life that she'd kept dodging and fighting, determined to make the most of who she was and what she could be. That took amazing strength of character, in Michael's opinion, and he admired her for it. To keep picking herself up and moving on from where she wasn't wanted, and find joy in something else…that was something very few people could do.

As he waited for Lucy to compose herself, his mind raced back over the past few weeks, picking up clues he'd missed. The mistake about chilli crab being on the menu that first day; her habit of choosing specials that were verbally listed by a waiter, when they were dining out, or observing what other people were eating and asking for the same; her panic at the idea of taking on Elizabeth's job as his PA, with Ellie staunchly supporting her, protecting her younger sister from being embarrassed by her disability.

He understood so much more about Lucy now: why she had been the one to drop out of school to nurse her mother, why she'd taken up hands-on jobs rather than desk ones, why few of them lasted very long, why advancement in any kind of serious career would be unlikely for her. The bookwork would be too hard to manage. She'd done what she could, probably relying a lot on Elizabeth's support.

Her anchor…

No matter what happened Lucy would always have her sister, who could be counted on to never waver in her love and support. Michael could see Elizabeth in that role.

He recalled Sarah Pickard's reading of Lucy, and realised now how accurate it was. Being ditzy was a good cover for feeling inadequate, she'd said, while he'd scoffed at the idea of Lucy feeling inadequate about anything. But the dyslexia did make her feel that way, which was why she hid it. Sarah had also been spot on about there being not much self-esteem in Lucy. How could there be if people kept putting her down because of her disability?

'Lucy, I think you're marvellous,' he said softly, wanting her to feel good about herself.

Her lashes flicked up and her tear-washed eyes searched his for truth.

'I do,' he asserted more strongly, holding her gaze with steady conviction. 'No matter how many people have cast you adrift because of your dyslexia, you haven't retreated from the world. You keep on setting out on another path and giving it your best. That drive to keep going, to keep finding joy in the world…you *are* marvellous, Lucy.'

'But…' she frowned at him, a wary uncertainty in her eyes '…you must see I'm defective, too.'

'Who isn't in one area or another?' he quickly answered, thinking *defective* was a particularly nasty word to be attached to Lucy. 'Harry says I have tunnel vision, not seeing anything except what's directly in front of me. You're in front of me, Lucy, and I like what I see.' Michael reached out to her. 'Give me your hand.'

Slowly, she lifted one hand and put it in his. He squeezed it reassuringly. 'I don't care if you can't read or write. I like having you with me. Now smile for me again.'

It was a wobbly smile, but at least there was a glimmer of hope in her eyes. 'I can read and write, Michael. It's just very slow and painstaking. I'm much better at memorising things. That's how I got my driver's licence. Ellie drilled me until I knew all the answers off by heart and could recognise the questions. She's always been great like that, giving me help when I needed it. Though I don't like asking too much of her. I try to get along by myself.'

'You do very well by yourself,' Michael said admiringly. 'I would never have guessed you had any disability.'

She made a wry grimace. 'It's not something I want people to know. I'd rather be seen as normal.'

'You're way above normal, Lucy. You're very special.'

The smile came back. 'My mother used to say that. She used to say my smile was worth a thousand words.'

'She was right,' Michael assured her.

'It doesn't always help, though. The guy I was with before you—the control freak—used to make lists of things he wanted me to do. His handwriting was too hard to work out, so I just ignored the lists and did whatever I wanted. He got really angry about it and called me an airhead.'

'So you walked out on him.'

'Yes. I guess I could have explained, told him about the dyslexia, but I don't like abusive people. My father was very abusive to my mother.' She shook her head. 'I don't want that in my life.'

Michael nodded. 'Quite right! It's not acceptable.'

She beamed a brilliant smile at him and there was sunshine back in the room.

Knowing what he now knew, he should have decked that guy in the men's room for calling Lucy an airhead, though violence wasn't acceptable, either. Instead of standing up for her, he'd been distracted by the sexual angle, which had led him into frog territory. Never again, he silently vowed. No man would like losing Lucy, and bruised egos undoubtedly prompted trying to damage her in the eyes of any other man she favoured.

Michael wondered how much abuse she had suffered because of her dyslexia. 'Your school years must have been hard, Lucy,' he said sympathetically, thinking of teachers who might not have spotted her disability for quite a while, and other kids calling her stupid.

'Yes and no. I was good at sports, which helped, winning me some approval for what I could do, and I did make friends who stuck by me. But schoolwork was a nightmare and I copped some bullying, which was fairly nasty. I was an easy target for those who liked to feel superior.'

'Tell me about it,' he urged, wanting her to unload all she had kept inside and be free of it with him.

Lucy could hardly believe that Michael was so accepting of her disability, not seeming to see any wrong in her at all. He kept encouraging her to talk about it, the problems it had caused her, how she had skirted around a lot of them. She made fun of some of the situations, and it was strangely exhilarating to laugh together about them. Other more distressing experiences drew nothing but sympathy from him, even admiration at how well she'd survived them, not letting them destroy her spirit to find pleasures to enjoy.

They talked all day, and when Lucy finally left Michael, she was almost on a giddy high from sheer happiness. The sense of freedom from having to keep her dyslexia hidden from him was so exhilarating she wanted to dance and whirl around and clap her hands.

Michael liked her as she was.

He might even love her as she was.

And he was very definitely a prince.

CHAPTER SIXTEEN

LUCY WAS IN THE habit of going straight from work to visit Michael. She did not stay long on Thursday evening because Harry was there, making arrangements about Michael's release from hospital on Friday, and Ellie had returned from the island, satisfied that the new manager could handle everything. It had been almost three weeks since she'd seen her sister and was eager to hear all her news and share her own.

Ellie was in the kitchen making a salad when she arrived home. 'Hi, Lucy!' she greeted her with a smile. 'Have you eaten?'

'No. Is there enough for two?'

'Sure! There wasn't much food here so I shopped.'

'I've been with Michael most of the time.'

'How is he today?'

'Still in considerable discomfort but he can manage with a walking stick so they're letting him out tomorrow.'

She nodded. 'Harry told me. I'll be helping in the office until Michael's ready to take over again. I'll train my replacement, too, make sure there's someone competent to assist him when I'm gone.'

'That's good of you, Ellie. Do you have some idea of what you want to do after that?'

'Oh yes!' She grinned. 'There's a bottle of Sauvignon Blanc in the fridge. How about you open it and we'll drink to the future?'

Lucy was happy to see her sister in such high spirits. The month on the island had made a big difference to her. Or Harry had. She opened the bottle of wine, filled two glasses and handed one to her sister. 'Is it a bright future with Harry?' she asked hopefully.

'He's asked me to marry him. And I'm going to, Lucy.'

'Oh, that's great news!' Lucy put down her glass to give Ellie a big hug. 'I'm so happy for you!'

'I'm happy, too. I really believe we're right together.'

Her eyes sparkled. Her skin glowed. Love was beaming out of her. Lucy's heart swelled with joy for her sister, who truly deserved a good man who would always care for her.

Ellie eased back from the hug to give her a searching look. 'How's it going with Michael?'

'Hey! You're not to worry about that. I want you and Harry to ride off into the sunset together without a care in the world. You promised not to let me get in the way, remember?'

'Yes, and I won't, but I'm not about to stop caring about you. I take it you're still in love with him.'

'Oh, I love him to bits and I think he cares about me, too. Though this accident has sort of interrupted things.'

'Lucy, it needs to be more than great sex.'

'I know.' But he hadn't yet remembered asking her

about sex with other men, and that might raise its ugly head again.

'When you phoned me last Sunday, you said he had no problem with your dyslexia. That's good, isn't it?'

'It's amazing! I hated having to reveal it but he was unbelievably nice to me about it. And it's such a relief to have it out in the open, not having to hide it.'

'Then it's made no difference to how he treats you.'

'None at all. I love being with him, Ellie.'

'Well, from what Harry tells me, he loves being with you, too.' Her face relaxed into a smile. 'Who knows? We might all end up in one happy family.'

'We might,' Lucy agreed, but she couldn't quite bring herself to believe it.

Having a lovely fantasy was one thing. Having it become reality was quite another. As much as she loved Michael, marriage was something else. Michael Finn was the kind of man who would want children, and although he admired how she had managed her life with dyslexia, she didn't think he'd want his own children to be afflicted by the disability.

There was no guarantee she wouldn't pass it on to any baby she had. She had kept pushing that unpalatable truth aside in the pleasure of having a wonderful relationship with an absolute prince but it was never going to go away. It was okay for Ellie to have a family. She didn't have the faulty gene. And Lucy was delighted that this was now a solid prospect for her sister with Harry.

As for herself, she had decided long ago that having children was not a fair option so a marriage with family was not going to happen. She thought living together was fine as long as both people were content with the situation. So far none of her relationships had proceeded to that level of acceptance of each other. She would love to be with Michael all the time but the wish for an always future with him was probably a dream that wouldn't come true.

However, she was not about to give up feeling happy with him as long as he felt happy with her. Live each day as it comes, she kept telling herself. One never knew how long a life would be. Michael's accident was a sober reminder of that truth.

As the days went by in the third week since the accident, far from feeling happy with them, Lucy began to panic about the non-arrival of her period. She was never late. The contraceptive pill she used kept her right on schedule with her monthly cycle. Except there was one night when she hadn't taken it—the night of the ball when she'd been too sick to think of it. Then with the shock of Michael's accident, she hadn't thought of taking a morning-after pill, either.

After their splendid lunch at Thala Lodge, they'd made love for hours before parting to dress up for the ball. That long and late sexy afternoon now loomed as the big danger. Yet surely, surely, fate couldn't be so unkind to punish her with an unplanned pregnancy because of one night's unlucky illness. She'd always been so obsessively careful, mindful of her disability and also of the misery an unplanned pregnancy had caused her mother, leading her into an unhappy marriage. It wasn't fair that this should happen to her.

By the fourth week, Lucy couldn't keep pushing the issue aside, couldn't keep desperately hoping this was simply some glitch in her system which would soon correct itself. She steeled herself to take a pregnancy test, needing to know if it was positive or negative. Living in this uncertainty was draining her of any joy in life. Michael had even queried if she was under stress at work. It was growing impossible to be her normal self.

She bought the test kit, rose early the next morning, shut herself in the bathroom and did what she had to do, fiercely willing the result to be negative. She held her breath as she watched the chemicals react. Her heart was a painful hammer in her chest. Her mind chanted *please, please, please...*

There was no kind fate.

As she stared at the positive result the blood drained from her face and the bottom fell out of her world. The shock of it was overwhelming. She fumbled the lid of the toilet down and sat on it, bending over to stop herself from fainting, sucking in deep breaths to clear the whirl of black dots.

Her mind kept railing against the terrible truth. It shouldn't have happened to her. It wasn't fair. The life she had managed so far was spinning completely out of control. She was adrift, more deeply than she had ever been. There was no way back, no way forward that wasn't a frightening blur.

When she felt strong enough she picked up all evidence of the pregnancy kit, took it to her bedroom and hid it in her wardrobe. Her first instinct was always to hide problems. This one was too big to be faced yet. She climbed back into bed, pulled the bedclothes over her head and curled up in the foetal position, wishing she'd never been born.

Time passed in a fog of misery.

Ellie called out to her but she couldn't bring herself to answer. She wanted everything to just go away. Her sister did not oblige, knocking on her door, coming in, asking what was wrong.

'Sick. Not going to work,' she mumbled. 'Tell Michael I can't visit him today.'

'What kind of sick?' Ellie asked worriedly. 'Can I get you anything?'

'No. Just go, Ellie. I want to sleep it off.'

'Well, call me if you need me,' Ellie pressed.

'Mmmh…'

She couldn't *need* Ellie with this. It would spoil what should be a happy time for her sister. It had to be kept hidden, at least until after Ellie's wedding to Harry. Even then, she wouldn't want to be a burden on their marriage.

This pregnancy made everything so difficult.

Especially with Michael being Harry's brother.

Her mind shied away from thinking about Michael. If she told him about the pregnancy and he felt obliged to offer marriage she would hate it, hate it, hate it. It was impossible to see anything working well in these circumstances. Besides, he might doubt it was his child, and she would hate that, too.

Tomorrow she might be able to come to some decision about him. Until she could work it out sensibly it was better not to talk to him at all, so she reached out to her bedside table and switched off her mobile phone, needing to prevent him from calling to ask how she was. She needed time to come to grips with everything.

Michael hated being incapacitated. He could move around his apartment—slowly—and do quite a bit for himself—

slowly—but until his right arm and ribs mended, he was useless in the office. He was trying to wean himself off pain-killers, too, which meant he was in fairly constant discomfort. At least he wasn't so concerned about what was happening with his business now that Elizabeth was here helping Harry. She wouldn't miss a thing, never had.

Though it did amaze him that Harry had decided to marry her. He'd had no idea that the attraction had gone so deep. On either side. He remembered Elizabeth being irritated by Harry's flirting and Harry had definitely considered her a challenge he wanted to win, but it was still a surprise that they felt so much for each other. A good surprise. He had no problem with Elizabeth being his sister-in-law. She was a very admirable woman—Lucy's anchor—responsible, trustworthy, caring, and very smart. Harry had made a fine choice for a lifelong partner.

It had actually spurred him into considering Lucy in the same light for himself. She was very different to her older sister, more endearing in lots of ways. He admired the core of strength underneath her vulnerabilities and she was certainly very caring. Smart, too. Dyslexia didn't limit her intelligence. He knew he wanted her in his life, but his life was abnormal at the moment. This was not the time to be considering a future with anyone.

He spent an hour browsing through some brochures on new fishing gear, having spread them out on the dining-table for easy access. At ten o'clock Elizabeth entered the apartment, bringing his coffee and chocolate muffin from the cafe on the ground floor, as she'd done every day when she'd been working for him.

'How are you doing this morning?' she asked brightly.

'Well enough,' he answered, smiling over their old routine. He'd resigned himself to finding a replacement for her but he doubted anyone could be as good.

'Lucy's not so well,' she remarked, setting the coffee and muffin on the table next to his left hand. 'Must have caught some bug or other. I left her in bed, too sick to go to work, so she won't be coming around to visit you today.'

He frowned over this news. 'I thought she wasn't quite herself the last couple of days. No joy bubbling over. I'll give her a call.'

'Leave it for a while, Michael. She said she wanted to sleep it off.'

'Okay. Thanks for the coffee.'

He waited until lunch time to call Lucy but couldn't get through to her. Her phone was dead. It stayed dead well into the afternoon. It concerned him that she felt too sick to want any communication with anyone. He remembered the yellow rose she had brought him in hospital to make him feel better and on impulse, made a call to Jack Pickard.

'It's Michael Finn, Jack. I have a favour to ask.'

'Ask away, Mickey,' he invited cheerily.

'You know the Pal Joey rose Lucy admired when we were over on the island. Do you happen to have one in bloom?'

'Several. Sarah was commenting on them this morning.'

'Would you cut one for Lucy? I'll send a helicopter over to have it collected. If you'd have it ready to go…?'

'I'll meet the helicopter with it myself,' he promised. 'Lovely girl, Lucy.'

'Yes, she is. Thanks, Jack. It should arrive within the hour.'

He immediately set about making the arrangements required to have the rose delivered to his office before five o'clock, then called Elizabeth to let her know to expect it.

'I want you to take it home to Lucy. Tell her it's from me to make her feel better and ask her to call me. Okay?'

'Will do,' she promised. 'Nice gesture, Michael. I'm sure Lucy will appreciate it.'

It left him smiling. Hopefully Lucy would be well enough to chat to him tonight. She made him forget about pain. He badly missed having sex with her and frequently cursed his broken bones for making him inactive on that front. Four weeks down and probably another four to go, he told himself, determined on making the fastest possible recovery. He just had to be patient. Lucy was still there for him, despite his blunder at the ball.

Lucy remained hiding in bed when her sister came home. Earlier in the day she'd cried herself to sleep and although that merciful oblivion was no longer her friend she was trying to hang onto it, dozing on and off, not ready to face what had to be faced. She heard her door open and Ellie coming into the bedroom, moving quietly so as not to disturb her. She kept her eyes closed, not wanting to be questioned.

'Are you awake?' Ellie asked softly. 'I've brought you a cup of tea and a rose from Michael.'

A rose?

Lucy's mind was in such a mess, it clutched wildly at the hope that Michael truly loved her and would love her no matter what! She hitched herself up, eyes opened wide, heart thumping, only to see Ellie setting down a yellow rose in the same glass vase she had used to take her gift to Michael in the hospital.

Yellow, not red.

Not red for love.

Tears welled into her eyes so fast they overflowed and trickled down her cheeks. Her sister saw them before she could hide the emotional eruption. There was no escape from her immediate concern. Even as she flopped back down on the pillow and closed her eyes Ellie was sitting on the bed beside her, stroking her forehead, asking, 'What's wrong, Lucy?'

'Nothing,' she muttered.

'I don't believe you. Tell me what it is.'

'Just sick.'

'Sick with what? Your forehead isn't hot so you're not running a fever. And why have you got your phone switched off? Neither I nor Michael could reach you today.'

'Didn't want to be reached. Leave me alone, Ellie,' she said plaintively. 'I'm not up to talking.'

'You're hiding, Lucy,' came the voice of certainty.

'No. Just sick.'

'You're sick because you're bottling something up. You've done this before, going into retreat and churning over stuff you don't want to tell me about.'

'Please…let me be, Ellie,' she begged, quickly hiding her face in the pillow to stop the quizzing.

Her sister huffed in frustration. 'Well, at least call

Michael and thank him for the rose. He went to a great deal of trouble and expense to get it for you.'

'It's the wrong colour,' she mumbled into the pillow, tears gushing again.

'What do you mean…the wrong colour?' Ellie continued to probe. 'Michael said it was a special rose you particularly liked. He actually called Jack Pickard for one he'd grown over on the island and had it flown to Cairns by helicopter so I could put it here for you to smell. Now that deserves a thank you call from you, Lucy,' she declared with firm authority. 'I don't care how sick you are over whatever you're sick about. I'm switching your mobile on now and…'

'Don't!' Sheer panic jerked Lucy up, her arm flying out to snatch the mobile from her sister's grasp.

'What on earth…?' Ellie cried in shock.

Lucy clutched the mobile to her chest. 'I can't talk to him! I can't!'

'Why not?'

'Just leave me alone,' she pleaded.

'No, I won't!' Ellie wore her determined look. 'This has gone far enough. Tell me what's wrong, Lucy. I'm not going away until you do.'

Lucy bit her lip. It didn't stop the tears from falling.

'Tell me!' Ellie commanded.

Lucy shook her head. 'You can't fix it, Ellie.'

Her sister took a deep breath. 'Have you found out you've got cancer, like Mum?'

It was such a shocking leap she gasped, 'No…no…'

'Well, thank God for that!' Ellie regathered herself and drove forward. 'We've faced a lot together, Lucy.

It doesn't matter if this can be fixed or not. We face it together. So tell me what the problem is right now.'

Her sister…her anchor…

It was who Ellie was—through and through—and she was not about to let that part of their lives change.

Lucy's resistance collapsed.

This problem did have to be faced, and Ellie was right.

It was better faced together.

CHAPTER SEVENTEEN

MICHAEL PROWLED AROUND the penthouse apartment, banging his walking stick on the tiled floor, too unsettled to sit down and have breakfast with Harry.

'Ask Elizabeth to come straight up here when she arrives at the office,' he commanded his brother.

'Just because neither of them wanted to take calls last night…' Harry began in an overly reasonable tone.

'I want to know why,' Michael insisted. 'And I want to know now!'

'Okay!' Harry lifted his hands in surrender. 'As long as you remember to be kind to Elizabeth. It's not her fault if Lucy's sick and doesn't feel up to chatting.'

'It's more than that,' Michael muttered. 'I can feel it in my bones.'

'Probably because they're broken,' Harry muttered back at him.

'You don't know Lucy like I do,' Michael shot at him. 'I think she might be backing off me now that I'm getting better.'

'For what reason?' Harry eyed him in an assessing fashion. 'I know you've become used to her pandering to your every need this past month. I hope you haven't just been using her for that, Mickey. She is Elizabeth's sister.'

'No. That's not what it's about.' He couldn't forget feeling himself turning into a frog at the ball. Lucy wouldn't desert someone in need and he had been needy since the accident. She was big on empathy and caring. But now that he was well on the mend, other issues could be looked at and acted upon. He didn't want to confide something he was ashamed of to Harry. 'Please…just tell Elizabeth I need to talk to her.'

'Will do,' Harry finally agreed.

He had an impatient wait until Elizabeth did enter his apartment and the wary expression on her face instantly set off alarm bells in his head.

'Good morning, Michael,' she said so formally he sensed her keeping mental or emotional distance from him, which raised his inner tension several notches.

'Elizabeth…' he acknowledged with a nod, waving to an armchair in his living room '…have a seat.'

He propped himself on the wide armrest of its companion chair, directly facing her as she gingerly settled onto the deep cushion. 'What's happening with Lucy?' he asked point-blank.

Elizabeth held his gaze with a hard searching look of her own before calmly stating, 'Lucy is pregnant.'

'Pregnant…' he repeated dazedly, the shock of it sending his mind reeling.

'Because she was so sick the night of the ball, followed up by your accident, she forgot to take her contraceptive pill. Just one night she was off track, Michael. And unfortunately, you'd had a long session in bed that afternoon just prior to the ball. So that's how it happened.'

She didn't have to plead for his understanding. The circumstances were crystal clear. Knowing how obsessively careful Lucy was about safe sex, Michael could picture her deeply distressed by the outcome of this one mishap. He realised this was at the core of her withdrawal from him this past week. It was a big reason. A huge reason. But she should have shared it with him, not kept it to herself.

'Why didn't she tell me?' he shot at her sister.

Again the hard, searching look. 'Do you accept that you're the father, Michael?'

'Of course I accept it! Why wouldn't I?'

'Lucy thinks you might not believe you are. She thinks you're hung up on how many lovers she's had in the past. She said you asked about them that night.'

Michael gritted his teeth, knowing he'd painted himself as a frog, savagely wishing he could change the green into unblemished white.

Elizabeth sucked in a quick breath and continued, 'If it's a concern that will always be on your mind…'

'No!' He sliced the air with his hand in emphatically negative dismissal. 'It was prompted by what other men had said about Lucy but virtually at the moment I was asking the question I realised it was irrelevant to me. Irrelevant to us. And I've regretted bringing it up ever since.'

Elizabeth heaved a huge sigh of relief. 'Well, I'm glad we don't have that problem. I couldn't like you if you thought badly of my sister.'

'I don't. I love your sister, Elizabeth.'

The word slid straight out of his mouth before he'd even realised how true it was.

It evoked a doubtful look. 'Lucy doesn't know that, Michael, and to us *love* is a big word. Please don't use it lightly. Not in this situation.'

'I'll tell her. We'll work it out,' he asserted strongly.

Another sigh. Another doubtful look. 'You know about Lucy's dyslexia. She never planned to marry. Never planned to have children.'

Horror speared into his mind. 'She's not thinking of having an abortion?'

'No. Lucy has too much respect for life to choose that route, but she is upset about the possibility that she'll pass the disability on to her child. And she thinks you might not welcome a…a less than perfect child.'

The mountain of Lucy's vulnerabilities was rising up in front of him. She not only feared rejection from him but rejection of their child, as well. He suddenly had a very sharp memory of Sarah Pickard remarking that Lucy might think she wasn't good enough for him. In fact, Lucy had actually said so herself—*I know I'm no match for you.* This was a mountain he had to scale…somehow.

He shook his head over ever having considered her a possible gold-digger. That was so far from the truth—a million miles from the truth. She hadn't *planned* anything, hadn't expected anything of him, except that he would sooner or later turn into a frog and the pleasure of being with him would be over.

His jaw set in fierce determination. This frog was going to leap every mountain she put in front of him.

This frog was going to be the prince Lucy had wanted him to be.

'Thank you for being open with me, Elizabeth,' he said sincerely. 'I'll take it from here.'

She rose from the armchair, hesitating before heading for the door, her eyes meeting his in eloquent appeal. 'All four of us are going to have to live with whatever you decide, Michael. You must make it an honest decision. Trying to be honourable will only bring more hurt in the end.'

Honourable...standing up when he didn't really want to.

'Lucy and I will always have each other,' she went on. 'You don't have to be a part of her life. You understand? You must be honest so we know where we're going and can work out how best to do it.'

He nodded, seeing very clearly the crossroads where they all stood—two brothers and two sisters. Elizabeth and Harry were solid. They would move forward together. He and Lucy were looking down the barrel of very divergent paths if he didn't make the right moves—moves that had to be right for both of them. At the centre of those crossroads was a child who would tug at all of them, making the paths intersect throughout the future, causing conflict or bringing joy.

Elizabeth was at the door, about to open it, when he thought to ask her, 'How did Lucy respond to the Pal Joey rose you took home with you yesterday?'

Her reply was preceded by a wry grimace. 'She burst into tears. When I asked what was wrong she said it was the wrong colour.'

It made no sense to him. 'It's always yellow.'

Elizabeth sighed, her eyes sad as she answered, 'I think Lucy wanted a red rose from you, Michael.'

'Red...' he repeated, not immediately understanding.

'For love,' she spelled out. 'But please don't give her one unless you truly, truly mean it.'

She left, having made the situation with all its complications as clear as she could.

A great PA, Michael thought.

Then he turned his mind to Lucy and the child who would be theirs.

Decisions had to be made.

He wanted his sunshine girl back. She was dwelling in shadows, some of which he'd cast, others caused by the disability that had darkened many parts of her life—a disability she feared would blight their child's life. Somehow he had to pull her out of those shadows.

He thought of what Elizabeth had said about Lucy never having planned to marry, never having planned to have children. It made perfect sense of her having sex whenever it promised to give her pleasure. There was no moral issue involved, simply a need to feel loved for at least a little while.

Which was all she'd wanted from him. She'd told him so in the hospital when he'd more or less trapped her into revealing her dyslexia. She wasn't expecting to be loved for a long while. Her acceptance of that ruled how she thought, how she lived, making the most of every good moment.

He understood her now.

He understood it all.

And he realised how very critical it was that he make the right decisions.

CHAPTER EIGHTEEN

MICHAEL WAS COMING to talk to her tonight. Harry was bringing him to the apartment. Ellie was virtually standing over her, insisting this meeting be faced. No hiding. No bolting from it. No shutting her mind to the fact that this issue would touch all of them in the future. She had to listen and think very carefully about the decisions she made.

Having been instructed of all this, Lucy felt sick again—sick with nervous tension. She'd barely been able to eat any of the pasta meal she'd made for their dinner. Nevertheless, regardless of how she *felt*, pride demanded that she not *look* sick to the two Finn brothers.

She spent the hour before the eight o'clock deadline making herself appear bright and beautiful, determined to have Michael believe that the sunshine girl would pick herself up and move on, bringing up their child in her own way. After all, she was best equipped to do it, having firsthand experience at living with dyslexia. There was no need for him to concern himself about either of them.

Ellie had assured her that he did accept the child was his—no question. If this was true, he would probably offer financial support, which she would take. It was the sensible thing to do. Her own employment prospects would take a dive, being a single mother. In fact, whatever help he offered she would accept for their child's sake.

Having thought this through, Lucy was feeling a little more settled in her mind when the doorbell announced the brothers' arrival. Her heart, however, rocketed around her chest like a wound-up toy. They were early. It was only ten minutes to eight. She wasn't quite keyed up to face them yet. As Ellie moved to open the door, some self-protective instinct made Lucy step into the kitchen, putting the counter bench between her and the men who had changed their lives.

It wasn't Michael who entered. Nor Harry. Ellie opened the door wide to a delivery guy who was carrying a stunning arrangement of red roses—dozens of them clustered tightly together in a dome shape, and rising from the centre of this was a stick which held an amazing pom-pom of roses to top it all off.

'This is for the coffee table,' the guy said, moving in to place the gift as directed.

He was followed by two more delivery people whom he quickly instructed. 'That one is to go on the kitchen bench...'

More red roses, but fewer of them in this arrangement—a very artistic Japanese style.

'...and that one on the dining table.'

This was more a posy of red roses in a small dainty vase, perfect for its placing.

Fortunately Ellie had enough composure to thank the delivery people and see them out. Lucy was blown out of her mind. The sheer extravagance of the gift was dazzling. What it might mean…what it was supposed to mean…could she believe it? She kept staring at the roses…so many of them…red for *love*.

The doorbell rang again. Her gaze jerked to Ellie who was still standing by the door.

'Are you okay, Lucy?' she asked, her hand on the door-knob, pausing before turning it, waiting to be assured that her sister had herself under control.

Lucy nodded, grasping the end corners of the bench-top to hold herself steady. Her mind was a whirl. Her heart was drumming in her ears. Her stomach was cramping in nervous agitation. Everything she'd thought of saying to Michael had turned into a jumbled mess. Just listen and watch, she fiercely told herself. What he said, how he looked when he said it…that would tell her where she should go from here.

Ellie opened the door.

Michael entered first—still the most handsome prince in the world, commanding her total attention and tugging on everything female inside her. As on her very first night with him he was casually dressed; grey shorts, a grey and white striped sports shirt with buttons down the front—undoubtedly easier for taking off with his hurting ribs—scuffs on his feet. One of his hands was gripping a walking stick. The other held a single rose which wasn't red. It was pink and white.

Confused and hopelessly distressed, Lucy was barely aware of Harry following his brother in, pausing beside Ellie, speaking to her in a low voice. It was a jolt when suddenly they were both gone, the door closed behind them, leaving her alone with Michael and a roomful of roses that surely represented some kind of emotional pressure she would have to fight. Panic welled up. She needed her sister standing beside her, needed an anchor to stop her from being drawn into a bad place.

'There's nothing to be frightened of with me, Lucy,' Michael said, his deep rich voice pouring out in a soothing tone.

She swallowed hard, trying to clear the constriction in her throat. 'I'm sorry,' she managed to get out, gripping the counter edge even harder. 'I'm sorry for complicating your life like this. It wasn't meant to happen.'

'I know it wasn't meant to happen but I'm glad that it has.' He smiled at her, pushing one of the kitchen stools closer to where she stood and hitching himself onto the other. 'It doesn't complicate my life, Lucy. In fact, I'm seeing everything very clearly now.'

She shook her head. 'I don't understand.'

'Sit down and relax. We'll talk about whatever you don't understand.'

She unglued her hands from the bench-top, reached out for the stool and dragged it around to the other side of the counter to where Michael was seated, feeling safer with putting solid distance between them. She couldn't allow herself to be persuaded into doing something wrong. Having sat down she gestured to the roses on the kitchen bench beside her.

'You've never said you love me, Michael,' she flatly reminded him, her eyes searching his for any sign of insincerity.

'I'm saying it now.' His gaze held hers with intense conviction. 'I love you and I want to marry you, Lucy.

When we were on the island, I heard you say to Sarah that you'd never marry a man who didn't love you enough to give you roses. What you see here now is a promise there will always be roses in our marriage.'

Pain stabbed her heart. It killed her to say it but she had to. 'I won't marry you, Michael.'

'Why not?'

'It's wrong to marry because of a child. It's what my mother did, thinking it was for the best, but it wasn't. I promised her I'd never do that. No matter how good the intentions, it's bound not to turn out well.'

He didn't look at all deterred by this argument. He rolled right on over it. 'I'd agree that good intentions don't guarantee a good marriage. I think there has to be love between the couple involved for a marriage to work well and from what you've told me, I don't believe your father loved your mother. It's different for us, Lucy. I genuinely want you in my life and I believe you want me. Can you truthfully say you don't?'

'It's not as simple as that!' she cried, agonised by the need to keep on the right track here. 'Our child might have dyslexia too, Michael, and that wouldn't have been what you've planned for yourself.'

'I didn't *plan* anything for myself,' he swiftly replied. 'Somewhere on the back-burner in my mind was the hope that one day I might meet a woman with whom I could have the kind of relationship my father had with my mother. You're that person, Lucy—the woman who lights up my life. And I'm sure our child will light up both our lives, dyslexia or not.'

She couldn't let him just gloss over a condition he'd never lived with. 'You don't know what it's like…the confusion, the frustration, the realisation that you're not normal like other kids. The light goes out sometimes, Michael, and it's hard, learning how to turn it back on.'

The silvery grey eyes glittered with determination. 'Lucy, I promise you it won't be the problem it's been for you. We'll be on the lookout for it in however many children we have, get early professional help if it's needed.'

Children? He was looking ahead to having more than one child with her?

'I've been researching dyslexia on the internet,' he went on confidently. 'There's a lot that can now be done—programs that weren't available to you. But over and above that, we will both be *there* for our children. That's what counts most, isn't it, having a mother and father who love you, who think you're very special regardless of any disability?'

He spoke so caringly, Lucy's resistance to the idea of marriage began to crack. She wanted this man so much and she wanted her child to have a loving father. Yet there was another issue that could stalk and break the happy future together he was painting.

She sucked in a deep breath, released it in a shuddering sigh and looked at him with knowing wariness. 'What if you run into other men I've slept with in the past, Michael?'

His gaze did not waver from hers. 'I haven't forgotten I turned into a frog that night of the ball. I've been intensely grateful that you seemed to let me get away with it, staying by my side these past few weeks.'

'I didn't want you to die, didn't want to lose you, but I wasn't thinking there could be long future for us as a couple,' she quickly explained. 'You made me feel bad that night.'

'I know. And it's made me feel bad ever since. Please believe me when I now say I don't care if you've slept with *every* man in Cairns. If you'll marry me, Lucy, I'll always think I'm the lucky one for getting to keep you.'

The regretful tone, the vehemence of his plea to her…listening to him was playing havoc with her emotions. She so desperately wanted to believe him, yet… 'How can I be sure of that, Michael?'

'Give me the chance to prove it. I want to be your prince, Lucy. I want to love you, protect you, fight your battles for you, be your champion always. If you'll just favour me with your smile…'

The appeal in his voice, in his eyes, was irresistible, tugging at the corners of her mouth.

'…I'll conquer the world for you,' he finished with a flamboyant grin.

A gurgle of laughter erupted from her throat. This was all so impossibly romantic…the stuff of dreams… but it was washing straight through the cracks in her protective armour, swamping her heart, tugging at the love she felt for him.

He twirled the pink and white rose around in his fingers. The beautiful scent of it tickled her sense of smell.

'This rose is called Princess of Monaco. I want to give it to you because you're my princess, Lucy. I want to buy us a home with a garden where I can grow this rose so you'll always be reminded that you're my princess and I love you.' He held it out to her. 'Will you accept it from me?'

A river of emotion in full flood drowned the doubts

she had tried to hold onto. She couldn't stop her hand from reaching out and taking the perfect princess bloom, lifting it to her nose so she could breathe in the glorious scent. She couldn't stop the smile beaming her happiness at Michael—her prince. Her *true* prince.

It spilled into words. 'I love you, too.'

Desire blazed in his eyes. 'I wish I could race you off to bed, Lucy. I'd use that rose to caress every part of you so you'd be totally immersed in its scent and feel totally immersed in my love for you.'

'Oh! I do like that idea!' She gave him a saucy smile as she slid off the stool and rounded the bench to where he sat. 'We don't need to race, Michael. We can get there at a reasonable pace together. Will Harry keep Ellie away for a while?'

'Until I call him to come and get me.'

'Then we can take our time, can't we?'

'Lucy, I won't be able to…'

'But you can turn me into a rose garden and I can take you to the moon, my love,' she said, framing his beautiful face with her hands and kissing him with all the sensual promise of pleasure she could give him without any action on his part that might give him pain.

The fire she lit in Michael's groin demanded instant compliance with whatever Lucy wanted to do. He didn't care if there was some collateral pain. He wanted this intimacy, wanted to love her, wanted to feel her love for him.

She took him further than the moon. She made him burst into heaven and float there, feeling like a king, and he knew with absolute certainty that she would al-

ways be the queen in his life. She was the right woman
for him. She was the perfect woman for him—an exquisite addiction that would never end. And he silently
vowed that nothing would ever mar their happiness with
each other.

CHAPTER NINETEEN

IT WAS THE last day of her job with cemetery administration and she'd been asked to supervise the return of the repaired angels' heads to the memorial garden. Lucy was happy to be driving out to Greenlands, wanting to visit her mother's grave. Beside her on the van's passenger seat was a florist box containing the rose she planned to place there.

She arrived before the stonemason and was on her way down the rows of neatly tended graves when she spotted the elderly man who had planted the Pal Joey rose for his wife. She raised her free arm and waved, calling out, 'Hi, Mr Robson! It looks like your rosebush is thriving.'

His face lit up with pleasure. 'Miss Flippence! It is doing well, isn't it? And what have you got there?'

He set off down a cross path to meet up with her.

'It's a thank you gift for my mother,' she explained, pausing to wait for him so he could admire it and have a little chat. He was lonely, having lost his beloved wife.

'Ah! A Princess of Monaco,' he said as soon as he was close enough to recognise the bloom. 'Good choice! Wonderful scent!'

'Yes! My husband-to-be is going to plant one for me when we build our home,' she said proudly.

'Well, congratulations!' he said warmly. 'You look so happy. I wish you both all the best.'

'Thank you. I've never been so happy. It's like a miracle, finding someone who really loves you.'

'I guess you're going to visit your mother to tell her all about it.'

'Yes.' Lucy gave him a confidential smile. 'I think she worked the miracle for me. I asked her to, you see?'

His eyes twinkled at her. 'Then I'm sure she did. God bless you, girlie! Go on now and thank your mother.'

Such a nice man, Lucy thought as she walked on. There *were* princes in this world and she and Ellie were incredibly lucky to be loved by two of them.

Having placed the box at the foot of her mother's headstone, she sat on the lawn facing it, hugging her knees and tilting her head back to look up at the clear blue sky.

'If you're looking down at me, Mum, I hope you can see how magically everything has turned out since Ellie's birthday, and thank you so much if you've been a guiding spirit in it all. This is my last day on the job here because Ellie and I have a double wedding to plan and so much else besides. The four of us are looking at properties for our future homes and trying to figure out what will suit us best. And, of course, I'm three months pregnant and Michael doesn't want me doing too much so the job has to go. I'll still come and visit you though I won't be adrift any more. Isn't that wonderful?'

She heaved a happy sigh and lowered her gaze to the gift she wanted to share with her mother. 'This is the rose Michael gave me when he promised to always be there for me, my knight in shining armour. He chose it because it's called Princess of Monaco and I'm his princess, Mum. Remember how some of the schoolkids used to call me Loopy Lucy because of my dyslexia? I never thought I'd be anyone's princess. Sometimes I can hardly believe it but Michael really does love me. He makes me feel it all the time. And I love him with all my heart.'

Aware that the stonemason may well have arrived in the memorial garden by now, Lucy pushed herself upright and blew a kiss to the headstone. 'Ellie and I will be thinking of you on our wedding day. We know you would have loved to be there, seeing us as brides, and we know you would be proud of us. We followed what you told us—*Never commit your life to a man who doesn't love you and be absolutely sure he's a man you can love for the rest of your life.* We got it right, Mum, so you really can rest in peace.'

She lifted her arms high and twirled around in a happy dance, laughing with the sheer joy of being alive and being loved. She was Michael's princess bride. Nothing could be more *right* for her. And it felt so good.

So...good.

A miracle.

God bless everyone, she thought.

To feel this blessed was wonderful beyond words!

* * * * *

MODERN™

INTERNATIONAL AFFAIRS, SEDUCTION & PASSION GUARANTEED

My wish list for next month's titles...

In stores from 19th July 2013:

❏ The Billionaire's Trophy — Lynne Graham

❏ A Royal Without Rules — Caitlin Crews

❏ Imprisoned by a Vow — Annie West

❏ Duty at What Cost? — Michelle Conder

❏ The Rings That Bind — Michelle Smart

In stores from 2nd August 2013:

❏ Prince of Secrets — Lucy Monroe

❏ A Deal with Di Capua — Cathy Williams

❏ Exquisite Acquisitions — Charlene Sands

❏ Faking It to Making It — Ally Blake

❏ First Time For Everything — Aimee Carson

Available at WHSmith, Tesco, Asda, Eason, Amazon and Apple

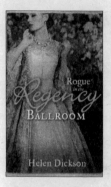